Bandido!

One hundred factory-new repeating rifles had gone missing, and if they fell into the wrong hands, the west would run red with blood.

The job of finding them and returning them to the Army fell to Shane Preston and Jonah Jones. But along the way they collected a rag-tag bunch of helpers, from a Mormon missionary to a disgraced, back-shooting sheriff. And even when they located the rifles, getting them back to Fort Dumas wasn't going to be easy. The Mexican outlaw Pedro Mantez wanted those weapons, and he didn't care how many innocent people his fifty-strong army of renegades had to kill to get them!

Bandido!

Cole Shelton

A Black Horse Western

ROBERT HALE

First published by Cleveland Publishing Co. Pty Ltd,
New South Wales, Australia
First published in 1967
© 2020 Mike Stotter and David Whitehead

This edition © The Crowood Press, 2020

ISBN 978-0-7198-3124-9

The Crowood Press
The Stable Block
Crowood Lane
Ramsbury
Marlborough
Wiltshire SN8 2HR

www.bhwesterns.com

Robert Hale is an imprint
of The Crowood Press

ONE

DESERT AMBUSH

They came out of the dusk, six spectral shadows moving slowly down from the long ridge in Indian file. They came silently, drifting past the contorted rim which jutted over the desert floor like a balcony, finally to rein in on the black lava ledge. Below them, the sand was a motionless blue-gray sea in the gathering gloom. The riders sat saddle for a while, letting their red-rimmed eyes wander to the north where the pass emerged into the wilderness.

"West of the rocks," Drew Paton grunted. The tall man's eyes had finally picked out what they were looking for. "Under the bald butte."

"Hell, yes!" Vinton grinned. "The bluebellies have lit their fire plumb in the middle of the desert. Shows how well they train 'em at West Point! Reckon some struttin' young fool of an officer's in charge, and right now he's figurin' how quiet things are—so they're sittin' round a blazin' fire plumb in the middle of Apache country!"

And Vinton finished his tirade on the military by spitting into the dust.

"A greenhorn bluebelly!" Paton quipped mirthlessly. "Well, in this instance, it's not the Apaches he'll have to worry about."

Vinton drew on his cigarette as he smiled at the outlaw boss. His face was stubbled, ugly as sin, with a long weal across his slab of a chin, and he had squinty little pig eyes. A thin, wry man, he seemed perched in the saddle on top of his bay.

"How many of 'em do you reckon there are?" Vinton growled.

They all looked at Dallas Jackson, and the former scout prodded his horse to the edge of the rim. He leaned forward in the saddle and fixed his eyes on the camp beneath the butte.

"I'd say half a dozen," Jackson said.

No one contradicted the balding scout. They used to say that Dallas Jackson had the eyes of a cat, and if he said there were half a dozen men down there around that campfire, no one disputed it.

"That kinda makes it one man apiece," Paton said, glancing around at the gaunt men who had ridden a hundred miles with him these last two days.

"Let's get it over with," Ringo growled. He was a bearded outlaw, chubby-faced, and he was hunched forward in the saddle, chewing tobacco.

"Vint." Paton motioned the wiry rider to his side. "Take Jackson and Ringo, and come at the camp from the dry creek. Moke and Davenish can ride with me. We'll cut down the sawtooth ridge and that way we'll have them in a crossfire."

"We take them all?" Vinton smiled in anticipation.

"All of them, Vint," Drew Paton confirmed. "We don't want no soldier-boys gettin' back to Fort Dumas to tell how we grabbed the gun consignment!"

Vinton nodded to the two riders assigned to him, and they set off down the narrow track which dropped steeply to the desert floor. The outlaw leader, Drew Paton, waited for a moment before turning his chestnut back along the dark ridge. Moke rode just behind him, with Davenish bringing up the rear. The dusk deepened into darkness, and away to the west, the crimson streak died in the sky. A wan moon showed amongst the pale stars. A breath of wind, a chill whisper, murmured from the north, and stirred the alkali dust.

The big chestnut led the way down the rugged slope from the sawtooth. By now, the campfire was plain to every eye—a glowing beacon just off the stage trail around which dark figures moved. The flickering shadows played over the white canvas of the wagon, and Paton grinned thinly. This was where the guns would be kept—a shipment of the latest repeating rifles en route to Fort Dumas, one of the most valuable freights ever to cross this brooding wasteland. And in just a few minutes, those guns would be his.

The outlaws clattered over the hard pumice, and now the wind began to rise to a low, steady moan. Like ghosts, the riders moved towards the campfire.

By now, Paton calculated, Vinton and his men would be staked out beyond the dry creek bed on the other side of the wagon. The outlaw leader dropped a hand to the rifle in his saddle scabbard. He drew the gun out, slowing his horse to a slow walk as he came closer to the camp. The cold, powdery sand muffled the horses' hoofs and Paton's smile widened as he surveyed the group of soldiers around the fire.

It was exactly as their informant at Laroo Crossing had told him—a lone wagon escorted by a small detachment of soldiers. The commander of the under-manned outpost of San Close could spare only a few men, even though this consignment for Fort Dumas was worth two thousand dollars or more.

Paton gestured to little Moke with his rifle, and the half-breed slid from his pinto. He'd recruited this part-Apache in a Mexican cantina two months ago, and Moke had already proved a good recruit to the bunch. He was an uncanny shot with a gun, and deadly with a knife at close-quarters. Paton nodded to the silent Davenish, and the man from Utah prodded his sorrel towards a stunted tree.

Drew Paton dismounted noiselessly. Gripping his gun, he crouched low in the soft sand. He could hear the crackle of the fire and hoarse laughter from the group as one of them spilled soup. Another

8

bluecoat soldier sat apart from the rest, and Paton guessed that he was the sentry but the man was far too close to the fire to see beyond the glow into the night. Quite obviously, these soldiers figured there was no danger at all right now. Maybe they didn't realize that they'd already crossed that invisible line and were now in hostile territory. Tomorrow, maybe, probing deep into the desert, they would be more careful.

Only, there was not going to be a tomorrow.

Davenish's horse smelled the picket-line and let out a long whinny and the sentry jumped up like a sprung jack-knife blade. Suddenly a deep hush settled over the camp, and two men leaped to their feet as the sentry stood there scanning the circle of darkness beyond the fire glow.

Paton raised his rifle and the bullet screamed through the silence and smashed the sentry's skull. The hapless man pitched forward like a spilled sack of flour, and even as the gun blast echoes thundered out over the desert, Vinton's bunch opened fire from the creek bed.

As a man, the soldiers groped for guns, plunging away from the firelight in a frenzy of activity. Bullets raked the camp from the darkness and, yelling to each other, the soldiers tried to level their carbines at the unseen enemy. Another vicious fusillade cracked out. Two soldiers rolled in the dust. One bloodied infantryman writhed right into the fire, and he rose screaming with flames licking his uniform, only to be cut down by Davenish.

The outlaws closed in, ringing the camp, pumping lead at the soldiers. A sandy-haired corporal crawled beneath the wagon and, callously, Vinton drew a bead on him. The outlaw's rifle boomed and the N.C.O. fell glassy-eyed over his smoking carbine.

The two remaining soldiers thrust their arms high.

"We surrender!" a white-faced youth croaked. "We surrender!"

Paton's face was a mask as he leveled his rifle at the young soldier. Three others fired at the same time and the two soldiers fell.

"Vint," Paton said, reloading his warm rifle, "check the wagon."

Vinton clambered into the rear of the wagon, and the fire glow played over stubbled faces and grim lips as the outlaws waited.

"Boss," Ringo growled, "Jackson's been hit."

Paton ignored Ringo's remark. He stood like a rock while the sound of creaking hinges came to them from the wagon.

"They're here!" Vinton cried elatedly. "Crates of 'em! Crates full of brand new rifles!"

The outlaw appeared at the wagon flap, his left fist clenched over a long black rifle. Vinton held the gun high, laughing in triumph, shaking the gun at the sky. Then he sobered as he handed the rifle to Paton.

"Just like Randell told us," he said, awe in his voice. "Beals repeatin' rifles! The very latest revolvin' Beals!"

Paton stroked the gun and then tossed it to Ringo. The rifle was handed from man to man and the outlaws squinted down the sights and tested the weapon for balance.

"How many crates, Vint?" Paton asked.

"See for yourself," Vinton grinned. "Ten of 'em! All stacked with Beals rifles—ten apiece! Makes one hundred rifles in all, and worth a damn fortune!"

"I reckon he'll pay well for them," Paton mused, climbing into the wagon to survey the loot.

"Double their value?" Vinton asked hopefully.

"Mebbe he'll even pay triple," Drew Paton smiled. "Think of it, Vint—six thousand bucks, or more!"

"A thousand apiece," Vinton said.

"More than a thousand," Paton said quietly. "In a couple of minutes, there'll be only five of us to share the loot."

There was a long silence.

"Yeah," Vinton murmured. "Too bad about Jackson."

"Hitch a couple of the soldier-boys' horses to the wagon," Drew Paton told him. "We've movin' out."

The outlaw boss climbed down from the wagon. The wounded Jackson had been carried from the darkness to a soldier's saddle blanket, and now the dancing fire glow played over his bloodied chest.

Paton checked out the outlaw's wound.

11

"Bad luck, Jackson," he said.

"Bastard got me—in the chest!" Dallas Jackson coughed up blood. His tortured eyes looked up at Paton. "Must have been—the last shot fired before—before those galoots jumped up—and surrendered!"

"He'll have to ride in the wagon with the guns," Davenish said.

"Ride to where?" Paton asked.

"Guess we'll have to get him to some doc," suggested Davenish.

Paton built a cigarette. Blood was oozing from the corners of Dallas Jackson's mouth.

"Jackson knows the rules," Paton said. "Don't you, Jackson?"

Jackson didn't answer. His eyes rolled as he stared up at the outlaw leader. A terrible fear was mirrored on his face, fear and bewilderment as he looked from man to man as they crowded around him.

"A wounded man would slow us down, give us trouble," Paton said tonelessly. He struck a match and lit his cigarette. There was no mercy in his voice, not even a semblance of pity. "Besides, it would be too risky to take him into a town where there's a sawbones."

Davenish and Moke straightened up. Sure, they knew the rules, but till now they'd never had to apply them. Beyond the fire, Ringo was stooped over a dead soldier, ripping a gold watch and chain from the man's fob pocket. He was pretending not to be concerned, but he was listening hard to all that was said.

It was Davenish who opened his mouth to speak, but it was too late. He saw the long deadly shadow of Paton's rifle in the fierce glow of the fire, then there was a sharp, sudden explosion. The echoes faded into the night, and the outlaws all stared at the body of the man who'd ridden with them so far. There was a small, neat hole between his eyes.

They mounted up in silence. Grim-faced, they waited for Vinton as he completed the hitching of the wagon horses. The half-breed, Moke, turned his head away and retched. Vinton flicked a whip over the wagon horses and the prairie schooner swayed away from the campfire. It was Drew Paton who sat saddle until the last moment, finishing his cigarette.

"Reckon he knew the rules," Paton shrugged, dropping his cigarette beside Dallas Jackson's body. "We never take a wounded man with us."

The wagon lumbered off into the darkness and the four riders drifted behind the swaying vehicle, its white canvas ghostly in the moonlight. The fire flickered, throwing its ruddy glare over the scene of carnage. Within a few minutes, a coyote howled from the ridge. Noiselessly, the desert scavengers began to pad down towards the stench of death.

TWO

TRAIL TO FORT DUMAS

"Mr. Preston!" The stern female voice arrested the tall man as he prepared to mount the stairs to his room.

"Yes, Miss Cloke?" The Texan glanced back at the desk in the lobby where the slim, willowy Miss Amy Cloke sat primly behind her guests' book. "Something troubling you?"

"You must know something's troubling me!" There was a ringing accusation in her tone. The lady owner of the Trail's End Rooming House looked annoyed, but Shane Preston told himself as she thrust out her firm bosom that this middle-aged spinster could under some circumstances be regarded as attractive. "That friend of yours!" the lady went on. "Not only troubling me, but every guest on the premises as well!

14

And, if my information is correct, every decent, God-fearing person in Durango Butte!"

"Jonah's that much trouble, Miss Cloke?"

The lady stood up. "Mr. Preston, I consider myself a broad-minded woman."

"You do?" asked Shane innocently.

"I'm no prude," she elaborated. "I believe in facing the facts of life, Mr. Preston."

"So do I, ma'am," Shane said.

"I turned a blind eye when that Mr. Jones of yours brought in whisky and polluted my respectable establishment ..." She turned and tapped the large, hand-painted notice on the wall which listed the rules of the Trail's End roomer. One of those rules stipulated that whisky, in fact any alcohol, was strictly forbidden on the premises. "I even said nothing when he drank in his room and left a bottle for me to throw out, but ..."

"But?"

"I draw the line at him entertaining, no, cavorting with women of ill-fame up there in Room Seven!"

"Ma'am, I'm sure my pard wouldn't—"

"He's doing it right now!" she said and her bosom heaved. "One of the guests saw him bring in that—that painted creature! I was out at the time, or else I'd have thrown her out, the baggage!"

"So you haven't been up to the room?" Shane Preston asked her mildly.

15

"Of course not!" Miss Amy Cloke looked shocked at the suggestion. "I'm a Christian woman, Mr. Preston, and some things I do not want to see!"

"I guess you're right, ma'am," Shane murmured insincerely. Maybe it would do Miss Cloke no harm to broaden her mind a little more. "Look, I'll go up there and speak to Jonah now."

"Thank you, Mr. Preston," she said. She even managed a smile. "At least you are a gentleman."

Shane acknowledged her compliment with a grave bow, and continued on his way up the stairs. It was the third day of their rest-up in Durango Butte, and by the looks of things, they'd outstayed their welcome in this rooming house. The tall man paced across the landing and glancing down saw Amy Cloke watching him closely. Shane cleared his throat and moved towards Room Seven. The sound of giggling came to him, and he feared the worst. Jonah Jones was probably up to his usual caper—promising some susceptible female the bonds of matrimony to lure her into his bed. It had happened before, and the drifter knew it would happen again, like night following day.

Shane barged into the room without knocking, and stood there with his hands firmly planted on his hips and a wide grin on his face. Jonah was seated in a chair, a towel wrapped around his portly form, while a plump, raven-haired woman was perched on the bed beside a heap of his clothes. A needle and thread was poised in her fingers as she stared round at Shane Preston.

"Don't you figure it's mighty neighborly of Helen?" Jonah stammered out, with an over-eager grin. "Offered to mend all the holes in my shirts and socks and—"

"Up here in your room with you as naked as a babe?" Shane demanded.

"I'm covered!" Jonah indignantly tapped his towel.

"I'm a respectable woman, Mr. Preston," Helen pouted. She would be older than Miss Cloke, well past her prime, but there was still sensuousness about her. "I'm here on an errand of mercy."

"Amen," said old Jonah, casting up his eyes at the ceiling.

"Jonah," Shane said, "you know the house rules here!"

"Rules—hell!" the oldster protested.

"No women in the rooms," Shane reminded him. "Now if we want to stay here another couple of nights, we just have to obey the rules."

"Jonah's staying more than a couple of nights, Mr. Preston," Helen announced proudly.

"He is?"

"Jonah's made a very important decision," Helen said, going on with her patching. "He's stayin' right here in Durango Butte."

"Is that so?" Shane remarked dryly.

"If you want to ride on out, well, that's your business, but my Jonah's not goin' with you," Helen said confidently.

17

Shane didn't seem perturbed. In fact, he appeared to be far more calm and collected than the wriggling Jonah Jones.

"So my sidekick's been roped at last," Shane Preston grinned.

"Sure has!" Helen said proudly, slipping off the bed and waddling over to where Jonah sat grimly clutching his towel. "Jonah's drifting days are over. He's met the woman he's always dreamed of, and now he wants to settle down. That right, Jonah?"

"Well, er—Helen, honey—"

"Congratulations to you both," Shane said warmly. "When's the big day?"

"Real soon," Helen said for them both. "You staying around for the occasion, or will you be moving on, Mr. Preston?"

"Reckon Jonah can get hitched without me here to hold his hand," Shane told her.

Helen ran her fingers through the white mop of Jonah's hair. It was a gentle caress, but Jonah winced as if she'd scalped him.

"I can see you two lovebirds need to be left on your own," Shane said. "But before I leave, a piece of advice. Do your courting outside the rooming house—it upsets Miss Cloke having ladies in the rooms."

Shane made as if to walk out.

"Shane!" Jonah exclaimed.

"Yes?"

"You can't leave me—I mean, us, right at this moment!"

"Wouldn't want to stick around while you're courtin', Jonah," Shane told him.

"Look …" Jonah gasped, frantically making signs at Shane and hoping Helen wouldn't see them. "Please—don't—uh—leave us right now …"

There was the sound of heavy footsteps on the landing, followed by a loud, insistent hammering on the door.

"Must be Miss Cloke!" Jonah croaked, reaching for his half-mended pants.

"Miss Cloke don't wear heavy boots," Shane said dryly. The knocking sounded a second time, and Shane stepped closer to the door. "Who is it?"

"Ja—Lieutenant Gooden, United States Army!" came the terse reply from outside.

Jonah let the towel drop and hastily scrambled into his pants. In a frenzy, he whipped his arms into his shirt while Helen's eyes lingered on the chest he was covering button by button.

"Come in," Shane said, after allowing for his pard to look reasonably respectable.

The door opened wide and a ruddy-faced young man in full cavalry uniform stood there at attention. There was a fine powdering of alkali dust on his uniform.

"Mr. Preston and Mr. Jones?" the young man asked.

"That's us," Shane said warily.

"What's up, soldier-boy?" Jonah demanded, working on the last button.

"Gooden's the name—"

"You said that," remarked Jonah, still in a fluster.

"Reporting from Fort Dumas and Major Cannell," the cavalryman said.

"Tom Cannell?" Shane exclaimed.

"Major Thomas Cannell, sir," the young lieutenant said. "I'm his adjutant."

"Tom Cannell a major!" Shane said, obviously delighted. "Well, I'll be!"

"Major Cannell is now commander of Fort Dumas," said Gooden stiffly. He added "And a fine commander he is too. sir. A gentleman and a soldier."

"Well, well—So Tom Cannell's finally made it!" Shane mused.

"Listen, Shane—who the heck is this Cannell?" Jonah demanded. "Someone you fought with in the war?"

"Tom and I grew up together," Shane said. "Fished, rode, and played hooky from school together. Even courted the same girl! We both joined the Union army in the war, but when it was over, I took up farming while Tom made a career out of the army. Haven't seen Tom in years."

"I have a dispatch for you, sir," Gooden said. He extracted an envelope from his tunic pocket. "Major Cannell learned you were in this town, and he sent me straight here with this."

Shane took the official-looking envelope from the lieutenant. It had been heavily sealed, and no one spoke as the tall drifter went to the window and opened the letter with his thumbnail.

The Texan glanced at the contents quickly, then read them through with more care. Finally he turned to face Jonah.

"Tom's in trouble," he said tersely.

"Real trouble, sir, I might add," the lieutenant said, studiously keeping his eyes off the buxom Helen who stood as quiet as a mouse.

"Well—spill it!" Jonah urged, jumping around looking for his boots.

Shane decided it was time he came to his sidekick's rescue. "Jonah, I reckon you'll have to kind of postpone that hitching day."

"I will?" Jonah grinned, then tried to look mournful.

"Major Cannell needs our services, Jonah," Shane said. "No—not just the major … the United States Army!"

"Oh, no!" exclaimed Helen, clutching the oldster's arm.

"My country needs me, dear one," said Jonah, waving a boot.

She nodded proudly. "But you'll be back?"

"You bet!" said Jonah and started whistling as he put on the boot.

"Lieutenant," Shane said, "we'll go over to the saloon and have a drink while these lovebirds say goodbye."

Gooden hesitated. "Guess I'm on duty, Mr. Preston."

"No one's gonna tell Major Tom," Shane grinned, ushering the young officer out onto the landing.

Shane walked down the stairs and paused at the desk. "I don't figure you'll have any more bother with my pard, ma'am. We're checking out."

Amy Cloke smiled. Then she put her hands to her hair, smoothing it. "Always happy to have you, Mr. Preston."

Fort Dumas was an adobe outpost originally built to withstand Apache raiding parties. It was a square, drab structure with walls thicker than two men standing together, and enclosing a dusty parade ground with some wooden buildings. The outpost rose out of the desert like a sheer canyon wall, and the moment the three riders turned a bend in the trail they saw its gaunt, sun-bleached exterior sleeping in the hot noon sun.

Shane reined in his palomino. Like its rider, Snowfire was streaked with red dust and the sweat of a long trail, and the weary horse relished the moment's rest in the short shadow of a lonely butte.

"Gentlemen … Fort Dumas," Lieutenant Gooden announced.

"And this is where you bluecoat fellers live?" Jonah Jones asked incredulously.

"This is where we do our duty, sir," Gooden said good-humouredly. He'd become used to Jonah's ways by now, after days and nights on the trail.

"Looks like a damn godforsaken place to me!" Jonah Jones grunted. "Shane—remind me never to enlist."

"I don't believe the army would have you, Jonah," Gooden told him cheerfully.

The three riders headed on towards the double gates at the entrance to the fort. A dozen soldiers lined the outer wall as they approached, and the gates were pulled open to receive the visitors. Shane joined Gooden as the officer urged his horse on and old Jonah toiled along behind, cursing his aged mare, Tessie, who hated to be hurried. They all rode in and the gates closed behind them. They were surrounded at once by off-duty troopers and a sergeant hurried across the compound.

"See to their horses!" he ordered.

Shane slid from his saddle. Even among these troopers he towered above them all. He was rugged rather than handsome, but everything about him spoke of strength. His face was rugged, his expression resolute, with a prominent jaw that enhanced his air of being indomitable. His eyes were steady but in them were shadows as if he had suffered much in the past. Such was Shane Preston, saddle-pilgrim and drifter—and one of the fastest guns in the West.

"Come with me, gentlemen," Lieutenant Gooden said.

The two drifters crossed the parade ground as more troopers emerged from buildings and corrals to look at them. Fort Dumas wasn't exactly the crossroads of the West, and visitors were few and far between at that desert outpost. Several soldiers were gathered in front of the commanding officer's quarters, but they stood aside to let them through.

A blocky red-headed trooper was on guard at the door. He saluted as Gooden strode inside, followed by the Texans.

Gooden motioned to them to wait while he entered Major Cannell's private office to inform him of their arrival, but with a broad grin, Shane clapped the young officer on the back and went past him, calling out, "Howdy, Tom, you old son of a gun!"

"Shane Preston!" Major Thomas Cannell rose from his desk chair and dropped his cigar into the ashtray. "Welcome, welcome to Fort Dumas!"

The two old friends clasped hands. Jonah sidled in past the disapproving lieutenant.

"Been a long time, Tom!" Shane smiled, his handshake warm.

"Too long. And this, I presume, is your friend, Jonah Jones?" Cannell asked.

"The same," Shane said as old Jonah extended his hand towards the commanding officer. "Been with me three years now."

"You're both more than welcome." Cannell indicated chairs, then glanced at his adjutant. "You did well, James." Then he added with a smile, "You're excused duty, Lieutenant Gooden."

"But, sir, I have a report to make—" the punctilious young man began but the major waved him away.

"Later, later."

"Dismissed, James!" Jonas Jones barked.

The lieutenant automatically came to attention, saluted and was headed for the door before he realized who had given the order. He grinned and aimed a sideswipe at the old-timer before going out and closing the door behind him.

"Wine?" Major Cannell asked them, opening the well-stocked liquor cabinet against the wall. Above it hung a huge map.

"You have such a luxury out here?" Shane smiled.

"We have everything at Fort Dumas," Thomas Cannell assured him. "A doctor, general store, school, church—even lodgings for travelers who seek shelter overnight. This is more than a fort. It's a home for two hundred officers, wives and enlisted men."

"And a saloon?" Jonah asked hopefully.

"We have a liquor store—yes," the major said. As he poured the wine, Shane looked past his old friend and out the window. Three corrals were positioned along the western wall, and alongside them, the stables. Single log cabins under the southern wall housed the officers and their ladies, and Shane could see several women gossiping on a shady porch. There was only one tree inside Fort Dumas, he was to learn later, and this ancient cottonwood fronted a long, mud-brick building where the enlisted men slept. Beyond the palisades, a heat haze concealed the distant mountains, and dust hung in the heat of high noon.

Major Cannell, handing them their glasses of wine, said, "God knows I'm pleased to see you, Shane! I had the devil's own luck. Did Gooden tell you how I found out you were in Durango Butte?"

"Your adjutant didn't say much," Shane said. "I—ah—I don't think he completely approved of us."

"'Specially me," Jonah said with relish. "I'm not exactly a military man, Major Cannell."

The soldier chuckled and sipped his wine. He was the same age as Shane, but looked a decade older. The years out here in this dust-bowl had taken their toll. His hair was receding, leaving a burnished scalp. His shoulders, once as straight as a lance, were slightly stooped, and when he walked, it was with the gait of a tired man. Shane remembered Tom Cannell as a lean, wiry soldier fighting alongside him in the Civil War, but since then, a certain flabbiness had claimed him, and his neck was jowled.

"You were mentioned by a stage driver who stopped off here for the night," Tom Cannell recalled. "His name was Betterman, and he'd been in Blanco."

The Texans exchanged glances. "We were mixed up in a minor ruckus there," Shane said nodding.

"A minor ruckus!" the major exclaimed. "You call cleaning up a town of outlaws that? Betterman told me all about it, which sort of added to my information about you. You see, I've followed your career with more than ordinary interest since we parted company after the war. I even know why you became a drifter, Shane."

For a moment, distant memories claimed Shane Preston. For a moment, time was rolled back to a small homestead on a spread in East Texas, to a beautiful woman called Grace Preston. And Shane's face clouded as he saw again that terrible scene—his wife brutally murdered, his home ransacked, and those tracks leading west into the wilderness.

Cannell interrupted his sad recollections. "You've become a legend in Texas, Shane—you and Jonah Jones! And it seemed natural when those guns were lost to call you in since you were so close, in Durango Butte. But it wasn't just my decision."

Shane drank his warm wine, saying nothing.

"As I mentioned in my dispatch, I have official approval to bring you in on this and offer a reward if you're successful. Shane, the United States Army wants those guns back!"

"You've got a lot of men here, Tom," Shane observed, glancing again out of the window. "Surely they could have been used?"

"They were initially." Cannell poured a second round of drinks. "I told you about the raid in my letter. Now I'll elaborate. The first we heard of it was when a rider from Alkali Flat arrived with the story. Alkali Flat is a small desert town fairly close to the place where the guns were lost. Seems someone there stumbled on the bodies of the detachment. Naturally, I sent out a platoon to the scene. The bodies of the escort patrol—what was left of them—had been taken into Alkali Flat. The only things which remained at the camp were the burned-out embers of the fire and some cavalry horses which had strayed in search of feed. Everything else was gone, including the wagon-load of Beals rifles."

"No tracks?" Shane asked.

"Sandstorm had covered everything. We didn't even know which way they took the wagon."

"Who do you figure 'they' are?"

"Probably some bunch of no-good owlhoots. My scouts did find tracks of a small bunch of riders, no more than six, up in a soft patch in the hills above the desert camp."

"In your letter you mentioned Mantez," Shane prompted him.

"I figure that the guns are on their way to him. Maybe you haven't heard of Pedro Mantez?"

"We've heard of him," Shane said wryly. "Reckon most of Texas has heard of the Mexican skunk! Comes from south of the border and raids north with his army of marauders."

"All fifty of them," Cannell nodded.

"Fifty now? Last time I heard, he had about thirty hombres riding with him."

"According to my information, Mantez has recruited more men," the major said. "Seems he has every wanted Mexican hardcase on his payroll. Wouldn't be so bad if he stayed south of the line, but the bastard raids north. He's left a trail of pillage, rape and murder halfway across Southern Texas. And if he gets his hot hands on those guns, he'll be doubly dangerous!"

"So you don't know for sure that those rifles are on their way to Mantez?" Shane mused. "It's just a hunch?"

"This I do know, Shane," Cannell stated. "Mantez didn't take them himself. He was raiding a settlement several hundred miles away at the time. My guess is a small bunch of owlhoots killed the escort party and stole the guns, and they took them to sell to someone in the market for hardware. Now, in my book, there're only two outfits who'd be interested in rifles such as those—the Apaches and Mantez. We can rule out the Indians—they'd like to get their paws on them, sure enough, but they wouldn't have the money to pay for them. But Mantez would have the paydirt, and that's for sure! They say the loot in his camp would buy 'Frisco!"

"So you reckon this small bunch grabbed the guns to sell to Mantez," Shane summed up. "But maybe you're underestimating this no-account gang. Perhaps they intend keeping the rifles for themselves?"

"A few thousand bucks' worth of hardware for such a small outfit? It doesn't add up, Shane."

Shane thought it over. Cannell was stationed here in the desert above the Mexican border. He could read the signs better because he was part of the life in this wilderness. He knew its men and their aspirations.

"By now, Mantez might actually have his greasy paws on those guns," Jonah suggested.

"I doubt it," Cannell murmured. "According to all reports, Mantez stayed in the San Cisco territory for a few days—but he's probably heading this way now—on his way south to the border, and maybe to collect those guns!"

"And you want us to investigate," Shane said. He twirled his wineglass. "You must want those rifles awful bad."

"Shane—if that bastard gets his hands on those repeater rifles and arms his men with them, all hell will be let loose along the frontier! God, it's bad enough having Mantez carrying around old army carbines, but with those Beals guns, he could terrorize every settlement in Texas!"

"We'll do what we can, Tom," Shane said, but he deliberately didn't sound over-optimistic.

"I'm sorry I can't spare any men to help you," Cannell said. "Apart from the fact that my platoon came back from Alkali Flat empty-handed, I've got another problem on my plate. Red Knife."

"The Apache renegade?"

"He and his band of warriors struck at the Long Pine Outpost two days ago—killed everyone there, including the kids. I'll need every man I have to hunt the renegades down."

"Reckon I could do with another glass of that brew," Jonah said, eyeing the bottle of wine.

Cannell obliged him. "There's not much for you to go on, of course—just dead soldiers and one other body, probably an outlaw's."

"Identified?" Shane demanded.

"The coyotes and the buzzards got to him first, according to the towners. They said even his own wife wouldn't have recognized him."

"Dead soldiers, no tracks, no gun-wagon," Jonah recited ruefully. "Hell!"

"Shane," Major Cannell broached the subject carefully, "the financial arrangement suggested in the dispatch—it's okay?"

"It's okay," Shane said briefly. "We'll stock up on supplies and then hit the trail later on this afternoon. Reckon our first stop has to be Alkali Flat."

Cannell extended his hand again and grasped Shane's gratefully. "The United States Army—and a lot of innocent settlers—will be in your debt if you can prevent those guns from falling into the wrong hands."

Old Jonah grabbed the wine bottle as Cannell showed Shane the big wall-map. Jonah poured a full glass and raised it to the window where the stars and stripes hung limply from its tall pole.

"Might as well have a real long drink before I ride out to do my patriotic duty," he said, nodded to the flag and tipped the drink down his throat.

THREE

THE DESERTER

The shadows were lengthening as the burning sun dipped towards the western rim of the desert. Shane Preston had supervised the selection of supplies from the Fort Dumas store, and now he and Jonah were getting ready to move out.

Standing beside his horse, Shane flicked the ash from his cigarette as Jonah came waddling out from the liquor store. Shane's sidekick needed to shed some weight, he figured critically. Right now he looked flabby, though in a tight corner the oldster could still show surprising agility for a man of his age. Like Shane, Jonah wore his six-gun low-slung and when the need arose, he knew how to whip that gun out with deadly speed. He stood only shoulder-high to Shane and his weather-beaten face was largely concealed under a snowy-white beard and topped by a mop of hair of the same bleached color. Folks often remarked that Shane Preston and Jonah Jones were the unlikeliest of saddle pards, but nevertheless, they'd ridden together for three years—ever since their first encounter in a border saloon. Shane would always remember that day. He'd trailed his wife's killers there, blasted one to hell where he belonged, only to fold over with the second murderer's bullet in his belly. The last thing he remembered of that saloon was the smiling, evil face of the man who'd just shot him, a face with a deep scar! The next thing he remembered was regaining consciousness beside a campfire, with the man who'd taken him there and tended him, grinning from the other side of the flames. His savior had been Jonah.

Ever since that day, they'd ridden together, two drifters moving across the open range. But one of those drifters had a mission. Shane Preston was hunting the man with the scar, the last of the two men who'd raped and killed his wife. One day he would find Scarface, and then his six-gun would kill for the last time. Until then, he would drift, hiring out his gun when the cause was just, always hoping that his trail would cross that of Scarface.

"Shane." Jonah's husky voice interrupted the tall man's thoughts. "I reckon we're about to see a little ceremony."

The oldster pointed over to the blockhouse along-side the main gate.

Shane tossed away his cigarette. The guardroom door was thrown open and a tall, blond-haired soldier was marched out to the blockhouse wall. He seemed to walk with difficulty. Major Cannell stood with three other officers nearby.

A bugler mounted the blockhouse wall and his piercing notes rang out over the fort, summoning the men on parade. Briskly they formed a hollow square and stood to attention.

Drums were beating a somber tattoo.

"Someone gettin' promoted?" Jonah asked his sidekick.

"No, Jonah," Shane said soberly. "I guess not."

"Reckon I'll take a closer look-see."

"Suit yourself."

"You ain't comin'?"

"I've seen it all before," Shane said.

A strange silence settled over Fort Dumas. The prisoner turned to face the rows of men. His face was drawn, and he had trouble standing to attention. Shane knew what the ceremony was all about, although he didn't know the trooper's crime. He felt a twinge of pity for him.

"Trooper Abel Dancer," Major Cannell boomed, "we are here to carry out sentence passed on you by court-martial. Have you anything to say?"

The trooper shook his head without speaking.

"Abel Dancer," the major said, in a voice that carried all over the parade-ground, "you have been found guilty of desertion in the face of the enemy and sentenced to be dishonorably discharged from the United States Army. Color-Sergeant!"

A rugged, weather-beaten sergeant stepped smartly forward. He barked an order and the defaulter took two paces forward. He stood, swaying slightly, at rigid attention. The sergeant took a bayonet which gleamed brightly in the sun. With one stroke he slashed the top button from Dancer's tunic. Dancer did not flinch, though his face was twitching. The sergeant proceeded to slash off all the buttons from the tunic and then the shoulder insignia and decorations.

All the while, two side-drummers were beating their steady tattoo.

When the ex-trooper had been stripped of his regimental insignia, Major Cannell spoke sharply to the sergeant, who gave him a long, hard look, then, without a word, put the point of his bayonet in Dancer's tunic and slit it so that it tumbled in a heap at his feet. Beneath, he wore no shirt.

"Turn him around!" ordered the major, and the sergeant growled at Dancer, who shuffled about-face in the dust. Now, Shane—with all the rest—could see that the deserter had been branded on the back with the letter 'D'. The branding had been done recently and the weals were not yet healed.

"D for deserter," said Major Cannell grimly. "The men responsible for this barbarism will be court-martialed." The color-sergeant stared straight ahead, no expression showing on his face. "Let all this company understand," went on the major, "there will be no more summary justice on my force. Abel Dancer—dismissed!"

Dancer hesitated, then stooped, picked up his tattered tunic and draped it over his shoulders. He was shaking.

"Dismiss the company, Sergeant!" ordered the commanding officer and swiftly the parade was disbanded.

Jonah Jones made his way to where Shane stood.

"Did you ever see anythin' like that?" His beard was waggling in agitation. "Drummed out—and branded!"

"You heard the major," said Shane tonelessly. "Those responsible will be punished."

"Yeah, yeah. But an off-duty trooper—that fat cook over there—was tellin' me Dancer quit his post and when his buddies caught up with him, they fashioned a brandin' iron and heated it up right there and then and marked that poor devil for life. How can you rightly punish men for doin' a terrible thing like that?"

"Ten days in the brig, a stoppage of pay, no more," came a voice from behind them. Major Cannell stepped up to them, stern-faced. "There is no punishment to fit such a crime—yet I would not dare lean too hard on the sergeant and the rest of Dancer's troop. What Dancer did was even more terrible—he let down his friends in the face of great danger." The major's face relaxed slightly as he looked at Jonah. "We live in hard times, Jonah. And the army has to be tough to survive. We're well rid of a man like Dancer." He added, "He'll go out on the stagecoach—due any time now." He shook hands again with both of them and strode off.

A dust spiral came sweeping in from the desert, and already men were mounting the wall. They could hear the distant drumming of hoofs and the churning of wheels, topped by the sound of the stage-driver urging on his team of tired horses. Shane and Jonah rode their horses towards the entrance, but the westbound reached the twin gates before them. With a flourish of his long whip, the driver guided his team beneath the arch and the dust-streaked stage swayed to the boardwalk outside the general store. The coach came to a standstill as the dust settled, and the driver, a freckle-faced man, leaned over to address the passengers as they prepared to climb down.

"Ten minute rest-up while the horses are changed!" he bellowed.

Shane gave the first passenger a cursory glance. He was a lean, immaculately dressed dude with a white silk shirt, ruffled at the collar and cuffs, and a neatly tailored broadcloth suit. A natty derby sat on top of his egg-shaped head. Jonah grinned at the sight of this elegantly attired man and then raised his eyebrows as a young woman joined the dude on the dust of the parade-ground. Like him, she was dressed elegantly. Slender, with classical features, she wore a pink bonnet and gray travelling gown.

"Quite a looker!" Jonah whistled softly.

"Let's ride," Shane grunted.

But it was Shane who suddenly reined in just as they passed the stage. He sat saddle, staring as the next man clambered wearily out of the stagecoach to stand beside the dude.

"Judson Woode!" Shane called out.

The stocky, middle-aged traveler looked around with a start, and when he saw Shane Preston, he gasped in surprise. And then he dropped his gaze to his boots as the rider urged Snowfire right up to him.

"You're a long way from home, Judd," Shane said gently.

"Home!" Woode shrugged, without even greeting the rider. "Where's that?"

"Well, for you I'd say home was Santos," Shane said.

"Not anymore."

Shane glanced past him to where a bronze-skinned young woman had stepped lithely from the stagecoach.

"Howdy, Lianna," Shane greeted.

The half-breed girl came to stand next to Woode, linking her arm in his. Much younger than Judson Woode, Lianna was a willowy, sensuous-looking woman, with raven hair and an olive complexion. She was clad in a shirtwaist blouse and tight Levis, and the curves of her full breasts and hips pushed arrogantly against the workmanlike fabrics.

"I could say you're a long way from your usual stamping grounds, Shane," Woode observed.

"On official business," Jonah joined in.

"The theft of the Beals rifles?" Woode hazarded.

"How'd you figure that?" Shane asked.

"I was still a badge-toter in Santos when the news was wired through. Some outfit butchered an army escort and snatched the gun consignment. Figure you're here to help the boys in blue."

"Getting back to you, Judd, why'd you take off your badge?"

"Had it taken from me," Judd Woode said morosely.

"Judd!" The half-breed girl clutched his arm. "You don't have to explain to this—this gunslinger!"

"Wouldn't exactly call him that, Lianna," Woode said.

Shane appraised him, sensing his embarrassment. "It's your business, Judd. You don't have to say any more—even to a friend."

Shane turned his horse. The former sheriff stared at the ground, and Shane's shadow passed him as the drifter headed towards the gates. Jonah urged Tessie alongside.

"Say—just who is he?" Jonah demanded.

"He used to be lawman in Santos," Shane said.

"Didn't know you had many badge-toters among your friends!" Jonah said accusingly.

"Ran into Woode while you rode south to visit that widow woman," Shane Preston told him.

"The widow-woman Walsh," Jonah recalled with a grin.

"I liked the badge-toter when I first met him," Shane said.

"His wife seemed to have a sidewinder's tongue, though," Jonah remarked as they reached the gates.

"She's not his wife, Jonah."

"Huh?"

"She was living with him when I passed through, but she didn't carry his name."

"Mebbe that's why they took his tin star from him," the whiskery oldster suggested. "Reckon we've both known town committees lousy with over-righteous folks. They might have thought that a badge-toter ought to set a good example."

"Maybe," Shane said.

As they rode under the arch they spotted Abel Dancer waiting in the shade for the stage to pick him up. He turned his head sharply away as if he didn't want them to see his face. But Shane dismounted.

"Jonah," he said, "give me your canteen."

The oldster obeyed and Shane unscrewed the top. As usual, the container carried something stronger than water and Jonah stared as Shane stepped up to the deserter.

"This might help," Shane said.

Abel Dancer grabbed the canteen and took a long drink. Jonah was reflecting, as sometimes he did, that he didn't really know this man he'd ridden with for three long years. For here was the man who'd vowed to kill Scarface, a man whose relentlessness drove him on and on even when the trail was stone-cold, a man who had gunned down many outlaws—yet could stop to assist a deserter. Such was the enigma named Shane Preston.

Shane handed the canteen back to Jonah. "Reckon the stage won't be over-long," he told Dancer.

And with that, Shane led the way into the desert.

"Two more minutes!" the stage-driver, Matt Starrett, boomed as he backed a big bay into harness with the new team.

Lorn van Elnin muttered under his breath as he sipped the coffee provided by one of the officers' wives. The tall tinhorn gambler had hoped for a longer rest-up here, for he certainly wasn't looking forward to renewing acquaintance with the dust of the desert and the swaying stagecoach. In fact, he was only taking this trail out of pure necessity.

"How much longer to Blacksmith's Wells?" Binnie van Elnin asked her husband.

"A day's ride from the fort," the tinhorn grunted. "That's what they say—though not having travelled this godforsaken trail before, I can't vouch for its accuracy."

"We shouldn't be travelling it now," Binnie said. She'd taken off her pink bonnet to brush back her blonde ringlets. "We ought to still be in Lanterny."

Van Elnin looked sharply at his wife. "For God's sake—hush up, Binnie."

"How can I?" she demanded. "How can I forget I've left my home, my friends, everything—all because you couldn't play fair and square?"

"They were poor losers," the gambler shrugged.

"And you were a cheat," she snapped. She shook her head as she watched the former sheriff and Lianna climb into the stage. "What a stagecoach ride! Two men and their women on the run! A broken-down lawman and a cheating tinhorn!"

"At least I didn't kill anyone—like that fool, Woode!" Lorn van Elnin reminded her.

"You just stole their money," she stormed. "Marked decks! Lorn, you were lucky the town just threw you out. If it hadn't been for that deputy, you might have been the main event at a neck-tie party."

"We're movin' out!" Matt Starrett yelled.

The gambler and his wife moved towards the stage. Just before she moved inside, Binnie turned her gaze up to the driver. Matt Starrett had been waiting for that look, and he grinned as she flushed. He'd had his eyes on Mrs. van Elnin ever since she and her husband had boarded the westbound, and by the glances she had furtively afforded him, he reckoned his interest was returned. The gambler hurried her inside, and Starrett chuckled to himself. This wouldn't be the first time he'd carried on a mild flirtation with a female passenger, and he was already planning to get to know her even better tonight at the way-station. They had twelve hours' ride to Blacksmith's Wells— half a day to the way-station, then the following morning on the last leg of the trail to town.

"Giddap! Giddap!" The stage surged forward and the fresh team pulled the coach towards the gates.

The west-bound swayed out of the fort and Starrett pulled hard on the reins as he saw the figure standing in his way. Starrett glared at the deserter with furious eyes. Cannell had informed him about this passenger, and the driver hadn't been keen to take him on board, but nevertheless he had agreed, especially as the major had said Dancer would be able to pay his fare.

"You loco!" Starrett upbraided Dancer for standing in the middle of the trail. "Why the hell didn't you wait on the side?"

"Didn't want you—to miss me," Abel Dancer said with difficulty.

Starrett looked at him with loathing. "Yellerbelly!" he sneered. "Haven't you forgotten something? Major Cannell told me you had some army back-pay on you! This ain't a charity stage, you know."

"How much?" Dancer asked.

"Thirty bucks," Starrett said unblinkingly.

"But, that's—that's almost all my pay! It—it couldn't be all that much! Fare's only six bucks!"

"For you, it's thirty," Starrett said relentlessly. "Take it or leave it, mister."

Trembling, having no choice, Dancer counted out the money and handed it up to Starrett. Then he climbed into the stage and sat next to van Elnin. The gambler regarded him distastefully, rubbing a silk handkerchief across his face and looking at his wife.

The stage lurched forward.

"If there's one thing in life I can't stomach, it's an army deserter!" the gambler observed. "It's an insult to have him travel with us."

Abel Dancer leaned back on the wooden seat, and behind him, the fort slowly receded.

"Like Tom said," Shane Preston observed, "spent cartridges and charred wood."

He stood up beside the remains of the campfire. It was a lonely, desolate part of the wilderness in the shadow of the two buttes. On all sides, the red sand stretched to distant pumice walls, and the only vegetation consisted of a few dead trees and a patch of purple, flowering sagebrush.

"So we've got nothing to go on," Jonah said.

"Someone from Alkali Flat found the bodies and took them into town," Shane stated. "Reckon that's where we'll head."

The drifters mounted up.

A soft blue-gray prelude to dusk gripped the desert as the Texans moved away from the scene of the massacre towards the northern fork in the trail. Recalling Cannell's wall-map, Shane rode along the base of the smaller butte and back through the pass. At the fork, they followed the well-worn mule track to where a long, rounded rim protruded over the wilderness below.

Here the red sand gave way to whiteness, and as they descended from the rim, Shane and Jonah could smell the tang of salt. The surface was hard, and their horses' hoofs crunched the whiteness like frozen snow. To the west, the sun dyed the salt a deep crimson. Here, there were no animal tracks, no birds, no bushes. For this was a dead land.

The trail wound through the white ridges and mounted a huge bluff. In the distance, lamps lit up the gathering darkness, and as the drifters neared the town limits, they heard shouting.

"Sounds like some sorta celebration," Jonah muttered.

"Doubt it," Shane shrugged. "Those folks sound angry."

By now, some of the lanterns were moving, carried by bobbing hands, and the yelling mounted. The drifters urged their horses along a little faster, and it was Shane who headed Snowfire first into the long, wide street which sliced Alkali Flat into two parts.

It seemed as if nearly every lantern in town was at the far end of Main Street, and almost all the porches and windows were wreathed in darkness. Shane reined in outside the grain store. Even the saloon was silent. In fact, one man had just parted the batwings and he was running to join the crowd gathering under a huge old oak—which seemed to be the only tree for miles around.

"Howdy, strangers."

Shane and Jonah turned in their saddles as an old-timer, maybe older even than Jonah, puffed away on his pipe on the grain store porch. This bald-headed, smiling citizen was perched on a water barrel, his knees tucked up almost to his bearded chin.

"Why, howdy," Shane said warmly. "What's goin' on down the street?"

"Oh, I'd be down there myself, but I've seen plenty in my time," the old-timer drawled. "Seen one, you seen 'em all, that's what my pa used to say—bless his memory."

"Seen what?" Shane demanded.

"This 'un is different, mind you. They say the feller ain't exactly a horse-thief or a back-shooter … or anythin' like that at all. But he must be gettin' his just desserts or they wouldn't be hangin' him."

"A hanging!" Shane and Jonah exclaimed together.

"Yeah," the towner smiled. "A neck-tie party. Didn't I explain it proper? He's due to hang at seven, and by my watch, the critter's got precisely one minute to stay breathin'!"

FOUR ⬧

LYNCH PARTY IN ALKALI FLAT

"All right, Lassetter—say your prayers!" the saloon-keeper, Josh Klagg, told him.

For the first time there was silence as twenty lanterns were thrust up at the prisoner. John Lassetter had been lifted onto his horse and his hands tied behind his back. A rawhide noose was biting into his neck, and the rope hung stiffly from a low branch. Holding the horse was stable hand Graber, but within seconds the sorrel would be released and helped on its way by a well-aimed slap on the rump—leaving the lanky prisoner dangling in mid-air.

"Prayers?" Beeve Franklin quipped. He was a lay-preacher in his spare time. "Heathens like Lassetter don't actually pray!"

"Listen—all of you!" Lassetter pleaded with them.

"Give the coyote his say," someone grunted.

"I've done nothing wrong!" Lassetter ran his frightened eyes over the mob. The flickering lamp-glow showed him their enraged faces, the righteous fury in their eyes. "For the love of God, you must listen! All I did was come to your town and preach the word of truth to you!"

"Word of truth!" The lay-preacher almost frothed at the mouth. "You came here spilling out damnable lies and heresy about a prophet called Joseph Smith and his angel Moroni and that counterfeit Book of Mormon!"

"They are not lies! They are the truth!" Lassetter wrenched his face around to plead with those on the other side of him. "I tell you, God has revealed his truth in his new prophet, Joseph Smith. I did not come here to do away with your religion, but to add to it, to give it new depth."

"And to lead our women astray!" Klagg reminded him. "What sort of religion is it where men have more than one wife? Now, I'm just a saloon-keeper, but I keep to the Good Book, and the way I read it, a man has one wife—not two or three or more, like you teach! God knows what might have happened if we hadn't stopped you! Look what happened to Betsy Underdale and Avis McVeeter—they both wanted to marry you, and they were so led astray by you that they actually believed it was God's will to share you!"

"I say we hang the Mormon varmint now!" Franklin roared out his hatred of heresy. "He is of the devil! His beliefs are of the devil! And he would lead our women to the devil, too!"

"Please—"

"All over the west, decent God-fearing towns have been hanging Mormon devils," Klagg cried. "If every town treated them like vermin, we'd soon be rid of them and their devilish ways!"

Shouts of agreement greeted the saloon-keeper's speech. Many of the men in the lynch-party weren't exactly regular churchgoers, but what John Lassetter had preached during the tumultuous days he'd been in Alkali Flat had so incensed them that hanging seemed too good for him. If he'd been some fiery tent-evangelist slating their liquor establishment and their gambling ways, no one would have paid much attention. But Lassetter was here with a rope around his neck because he was different. He not only preached unorthodox doctrines—which only offended those who attended chapel—but also unorthodox practices. He'd told them that God sanctioned polygamy, and had then proceeded to win over several ladies of the town to his cause. Rumor quickly spread that more than one lady had shared his bed, and at least two had expressed the wish to marry him and leave with him on his journey to Salt Lake City in Utah. It had seemed that the young, good-looking Mormon preacher possessed more than speaking ability—he had a personal magnetism which attracted the opposite sex like bees to pollen. Maybe it was this more than his strange doctrines which had rocked the town and made the men realize that John Lassetter was a threat to them.

"Say your prayers, Lassetter," Franklin snarled. "That is if you know any real ones!"

The rope tightened and Lassetter closed his eyes. The Mormon's mouth moved in prayer, but far from changing their minds, this display of devotion made their fury mount. To some of them, it was more than heresy that the devil incarnate should actually speak with his Maker.

"Make the bastard dance rope!" a miner yelled.

"He seduced my daughter knowin' she was just seventeen!" another fumed. "Changed her from a Christian girl into a loony eyed Mormon-lover! I want to see him hang!"

"Now!" the miner roared impatiently.

The brawny flour miller, Hammill, shoved a couple of men aside and raised his fist to strike the rump of Lassetter's horse.

And it was then that the two riders on the fringes of the crowd drew six-guns from their holsters.

"Hold it!" Shane's ringing voice plunged them all into silence. "Just hold it right there, gents!"

As a man, the lynch mob turned, lifting lanterns so the flickering light fell over the two dark riders sitting saddle with drawn guns. The irate townsmen had been so intent on the business in hand that no one had noticed the strangers drifting up to the old oak.

"Who in the hell are you?" Klagg demanded, his eyes bulging.

"Name's Shane Preston," the tall drifter told him, his gun steady as a rock in his fist.

"I'm Jones," Jonah supplied. The oldster had positioned himself just around from Shane, and the six-gun in his hand was pointed directly at the flour miller whose raised fist still hung above his head.

"You two are strangers," Franklin cried. "This ain't your party—so vamoose, damn you!"

"This man had a trial?" Shane said, ignoring Franklin's command.

"We've all tried him, and by the powers, he's guilty!" a twitching little man screamed out.

"Guilty of what?" Shane was deliberately making them recite the charges against Lassetter. He'd had experience with more than one lynch mob in his time, and he'd found that the best way to cool fiery tempers was to keep talking things over. "Is he a rustler?"

"Well, no …" Franklin admitted.

"He rob the bank?" Jonah asked.

"He shoot someone in the back?" Shane whipped in with another quick question.

"No! He did none of those things!" Klagg waded through the crowd. "But he's a goddamn Mormon!"

"You mean he's got a different religion to the rest of you?" Shane demanded.

"A different religion! His ways are of the devil!" Franklin was trembling with rage. "He's been seducing our women with his damnable doctrines! Now, put those guns away and let us get on with the chore we came here to do!"

"You!" Shane selected a pallid-faced youth who was right beside John Lassetter's horse. "Cut him down."

Shane's order was greeted with cries of baffled fury from the mob. Fists rose in the night. Franklin yelled an oath, and with his eyes on fire, he dropped a hand to his gun. The lay-preacher's six-gun slipped from its holster, and men leaped back as he lifted it with a trembling hand.

The tall drifter's trigger-finger moved a fraction and the explosion was like a thunderclap. Franklin whipped around, the slug burning into the top of his arm, and he tossed away his gun with a groan. A solemn hush fell over the crowd as Franklin staggered into Hammill's arms and wept like a child against his shoulder.

Shane thumbed back the hammer of his gun. "Anyone else?" he challenged. His voice was as cold as chilled steel.

It was as if the sudden gun blast had sobered them all. The sneer on their faces had turned to bewilderment and not one man dared let his hand even brush his gun butt. The two naked gun muzzles stared at them like twin cold eyes, and not one out of that lynch mob was going to attempt to beat those trigger fingers.

"Right," Shane smiled grimly. "Now cut him down."

"He's—he's a Mormon!" the saloon-keeper said feebly. "All over the west, towns are—are hangin' the varmints."

"You've said that before," Shane told him. "I'm not impressed."

The pale youth reached up with his knife and cut the rawhide above the noose. Lassetter's head flopped forward.

"The Lord be praised," he murmured faintly.

"His hands," Shane directed.

No one spoke as the youth sliced the ropes binding his wrists.

"By what right have you done this?" Franklin cried, nursing his bloodied arm.

"I'm no Mormon-lover," Shane Preston told the lay-preacher, "neither do I hold with neck-tie parties—specially since this man's crime is only that he's different from the rest of you."

Their simmering fury had died now. The drifters' intervention and the subsequent wounding of Franklin had taken the sting out of them, but there was still anger and hatred in their eyes. Lassetter urged his horse through the crowd, heading it towards his rescuers.

"We want him out of our town," Klagg fumed. "We want you all out, in fact—all three of you!"

"I wasn't aiming to put down roots," Shane assured him. "I only came here to ask some questions and happened on this neck-tie party."

Lassetter was right beside him now.

"Thank you, Mr. Preston," the Mormon whispered.

"What sorta questions?" Klagg demanded.

The men of Alkali Flat glanced at each other and then regarded Shane and Jonah with hostility.

"We're from Fort Dumas," Shane stated.

The towners exchanged furtive whispers.

"So?" Klagg shrugged.

"We're here making enquiries about the massacre and the theft of army rifles," Shane explained.

"The sold'er-boys came here a while back," said Klagg. "Reckon we told them everythin'."

Shane surveyed their lamp-lit faces. "I'd like to speak to the man who found the bodies."

A sober silence settled over the mob, and a couple of men sneaked away from the fringes and walked away behind the oak. One townsman doused his lantern.

"He ain't around," Franklin said tersely.

"What was his name?"

"Listen, Preston," Klagg spoke for them all, "you came into our town uninvited and horned in on what wasn't your business. Now we want you and this damn Mormon out!"

"Yeah," someone else yelled. "Leave us alone!"

"I want to know the man's name," Shane said coldly.

"He was just passin' through," the pallid youth said. "He ain't around anymore."

"The man who found the bodies must have noticed which way the outlaws' trail went from the camp," said Shane relentlessly.

"He said nothing," Klagg told him bluntly.

"Listen—all of you!" Shane's cold eyes went over the mob. He could tell they were hedging, maybe even lying. "I know that in your eyes we ain't exactly golden-haired boys after tonight's incident, but if those stolen army guns fall into the wrong hands, innocent folks could suffer—even whole towns like this one."

"He said nothing," Klagg repeated savagely.

"All we want to know is which way the killers went. We can then head in that direction and have some sort of hope of reclaiming those guns."

"This town wants you out!" Franklin growled.

"Reckon we ain't gonna get much help here," Jonah Jones told his sidekick. "They're so damn peeved we stopped their neck-tie party they're ready to let murderers get away with stolen guns that could be used to kill 'em."

Shane stared at the sea of dark faces. Maybe some of what Jonah had said was true, but the tall man doubted whether it was the full truth. Sure, they were angry at being deprived of their Mormon-hanging.

But they had just as much at stake as other small towns in seeing that a consignment of rifles didn't reach the wrong hands. But he saw no help in their faces.

"I figure we've outstayed our welcome, Jonah," Shane said quietly.

"You never was welcome, stranger," Klagg sneered. "Now get, and take that womanizin' heretic with you!"

"And Lassetter," a voice called from the crowd, "don't you ever come back. This town's a decent, Christian community and your devil-doctrines are something we can do without!"

Shane turned to Lassetter. "Looks like they're still in an ugly mood, Mormon. Reckon you'd better ride out with us."

"Never figured on riding out any other way," John Lassetter said fervently.

Shane and Jonah backed their horses, and the tall drifter holstered his six-gun. Although there was still baffled fury alive in this mob, the boiling passions had subsided as cold logic started to take over and hold sway. The moment for a hanging had passed. So had the moment for gunplay.

The Mormon rode between them and the trio headed out into the night.

"It was a definite answer to prayer," John Lassetter said, leaning back on his saddle beside the campfire.

"What was?" Jonah asked, glancing into the coffee pot.

"Your timely arrival in Alkali Flat," the Mormon stated. "I believe in prayer, Mr. Jones."

Shane finished his meal of beans and salt pork. They were on the white flats, just over a mile from town. Above them, the sky was a jeweled blanket, and around them, the alkali stretched like a moonlit sea to the dark outline of the desert ridge.

"Seems you caused quite a ruckus in Alkali Flat, Lassetter," Shane remarked dryly. "If you take my advice, you'd keep your beliefs to yourself when you're in a town like that one."

"We are missionaries for the truth," Lassetter told him.

"But spouting off about having more than one wife and actually persuading a couple of women to join you can be mighty dangerous," Shane said, trying to conceal a smile.

"Father Abraham had more than one wife," Lassetter said. "And furthermore, the saints today may indulge in the same practice so more children can be born into the household of faith."

"Havin' more than one wife sounds like a damn good notion to me," Jonah Jones mused.

Lassetter smiled broadly at the prospect of a convert.

"Mr. Jones—I can see the Lord is speaking to you."

"Huh?"

"Let me tell you about our founder, Joseph Smith …"

"Uh—"

Shane came to the rescue of his partner. "Lassetter, I don't figure Jonah would want more than one wife just to bring more children into your church. I reckon the old coot would have other reasons you mightn't approve of."

"Oh!" Lassetter exclaimed.

"What were you doing in Alkali Flat?" Shane asked.

"Actually, I lost my way and turned up there," the Mormon said, embarrassed at his own admission. "I took the opportunity to evangelize the town."

"You lost your way?"

"I was supposed to join up with a wagon-train carrying more of the faithful to Salt Lake City, Utah. Somehow, I missed the wagons, and rode into Alkali Flat."

"Utah's one helluva long way from here!" Jonah informed him.

"We're being persecuted all over the west because of our beliefs," John Lassetter went on. "Brigham Young has led many of our number to this place where there are now so many Mormon saints that persecution is not possible. It's the dream of every saint to reach Salt Lake City—and it was mine, until I missed the wagon-train."

"There will be other wagons going to Salt Lake City," Shane said sympathetically.

"I guess so."

"I suggest you ride to Fort Dumas and stay there until another passes through. I've heard of whole communities headed for this Salt Lake City place you mention, so you're bound to catch up with one if you wait long enough."

"That may be so," Lassetter said, "and later, I shall ride to this fort. But not yet. You see, I had a visitation."

"A what?" Jonah gaped.

"Oh, I've had them before," John Lassetter said airily. "It's usually the angel Moroni, and it was so this time. He's told me to stay with you two for a while."

"Now listen," Shane said sternly, "angel or no angel, you can't come with us. Our trail won't take us to your promised land—we're on the army's payroll looking for stolen rifles."

"Then you could need Moroni," Lassetter insisted.

"Coffee?" muttered Jonah.

A shocked expression flashed across the Mormon's face, and he shook his head vigorously.

"Certainly not!"

"Eh?" Jonah ejaculated.

"Drinking coffee is against the beliefs of the saints," John Lassetter said firmly.

"Well, that can be as it may," Shane said. "As for me, I'm not going without my coffee."

Lassetter turned his face away as the two drifters shared the coffee Jonah had brewed. There was a wide grin on Shane's face. Despite Lassetter's quaint beliefs, he found himself liking the man. Perhaps he admired the young man's cold nerve in descending on a town like Alkali Flat and preaching unpalatable doctrines to them. And maybe, on observation, he could understand why this Mormon traveler had made such an impression on the ladies of the town. John Lassetter had boyish good looks and a certain indefinable charm about him.

"The trail we'll be taking won't exactly be a camp town meeting—that's when we find the one to take," Shane Preston said.

"You did me a good turn," Lassetter said firmly. "The very least I can do is ride along to help you."

"On the other hand, from your point of view, maybe you'd be better off heading straight for the fort and waiting for another Mormon wagon-train," Shane suggested hopefully.

"Yeah, that's the best idea." Jonah smiled at his sidekick.

"But the visitation told me to stay with you," John Lassetter insisted.

They heard the whicker of a horse from out on the salt flat.

Jonah grabbed at his six-gun, motioning to John Lassetter to scramble out of the firelight. The Mormon needed no second prompting, diving into the darkness and dropping on his belly. On the other side of the fire, Shane Preston saw the silhouette against the moon. It was a lone horseman, motionless, a stark shadow against the yellow backdrop. Shane edged back from the fire, his eyes on the dark rider. Still the horseman didn't move.

"You out there in the night!" Shane called out to the shadow. "If you figure on coming in, then do it now—and keep your hands right where we can see them!"

FIVE

AN OLD MAN TALKS

Very slowly, the rider came out of the night, reining in just outside the fire glow. He was an old man, his head stooped, his face steeped in shadow under the wide brim of his battered Stetson. He was dressed in shabby clothes and there was no gun at his hip. As Shane stood up and walked towards him, the old man raised his face.

"I'm from town," the oldster said simply.

"Ebram Lemonnier," Lassetter said, jumping up. "I seem to recall I preached the truth to you and your wife last night."

"You preached to us," Ebram Lemonnier amended.

"Coffee's hot," Shane said. "You'd better join us."

The old-timer climbed down from his horse. His every move spoke of weariness, maybe defeat, and he slumped down beside the campfire as Jonah reached for the coffee pot.

"I wasn't in the lynchin' party, Mr. Preston," Lemonnier stated as Jonah handed him a mug of steaming coffee. "But I saw and heard what happened. I was in the shadows behind you."

Shane towered over him. "I hope you haven't come all this way to lecture us on how wrong we were to stop the hangin'?"

"I haven't come to talk about that, although personally, I figure the town's best rid of the womanizer." Ebram Lemonnier glared at the Mormon. "No, I'm here to talk about the massacre in the desert."

"What about it?" Shane asked him quietly.

"They lied to you, Mr. Preston." The old man gulped down his coffee and held out the tin mug. Jonah hastily refilled it from the coffee-pot. "The man who found the bodies and brought them in on his buckboard wasn't just passin' through. He still lives in town. In fact, he was one of that lynch mob tonight."

"So they lied because they were riled at us for stoppin' the hangin'," Jonah snorted.

"No."

"Huh?" Jonah stared.

"They would have lied anyway, even if you'd come bearin' gifts of gold," the old-timer said eloquently.

"Why?" Shane demanded.

"Because they'd be scared of reprisals if they told the truth," Ebram Lemonnier said. "They lied to the army and they lied to you."

"What is the truth?"

"The man happened on the camp soon after the raid," Lemonnier told them. "He—he said it was like hell itself. Blood, bodies and the smell of death everywhere, and—and damn coyotes rippin' one man's body to pieces. He took the bodies to town. Six bluebellies and one other jasper."

"That's what Major Cannell said had happened," Shane said.

"But nothing else was told the army—and there was something else," Lemonnier said. He stared into the flames, sipping his coffee. His eyes were vacant, and the hand which held the tin mug was shaking.

"What was that something else?" Shane prodded him quietly.

There was a long silence, but finally, Lemonnier spoke up. "One of those soldier-boys was alive when brought back to town. Just alive, but sinkin' fast. The outlaws who attacked the camp must have figured he was dead, and he must have played dead purty well. Anyhow, he was breathin' when he reached town. I remember how we all stood around him—just about the whole damn town. The sawbones tried to save him, but he died as the doc tried to slice out the lead."

"But he talked?" Shane urged him.

Lemonnier nodded. "Yeah—he just said a few words. He identified the outlaws who attacked the camp. He'd seen their leader's face on a dozen reward dodgers all over the territory. He was Drew Paton."

"Paton!" Shane exclaimed. "That weasel!"

"So you've heard of him?"

"Used to know him before he went on the owlhoot," Shane said, lighting a cigarette. "He was a smalltime rustler three years ago, and we were in Secundo when he was jailed for six months for running off a few steers. Reckon prison didn't reform him."

"It was Paton's gang who massacred them soldiers," Lemonnier asserted, "and took the guns."

"Which way did the trail lead?"

"The man who brought in the bodies didn't say—but it's not too hard to make a good guess." Lemonnier tossed the dregs of his second cup into the fire. "You've heard of Dry Creek?"

"Ain't that a ghost town?" Jonah frowned.

"Used to be a gold town," Shane supplied. "Just four years ago, it was the wildest boom town in Texas. A dozen saloons, gambling halls, and about a thousand gold-happy miners ... and their women. Now, they say, it's deserted. The gold lode ran out and as paydirt became less and less, the prospectors moved on. Now only the rats live there."

"With some human rats," the old towner added.

"Paton's outfit?"

"Half a dozen of 'em," Lemonnier said. "Although there's probably only five now. One of the men brought in wasn't a soldier—probably an outlaw killed in the fight."

"You seem to know a powerful lot about Paton," Jonah observed.

"Most everyone around here knows about him," the towner stated. "This is Paton's stamping ground. There's hardly a ranch house or outpost around here that hasn't had stock thieved by the varmint."

"And everyone knows where he holes up?" Shane asked.

"Most everyone," Lemonnier admitted. "Word kinda gets around in the desert, and more than one prospector has seen Drew Paton's bunch headin' back towards Dry Creek."

"And that's how you heard about it?"

There was a long pause and then, "Nope." Lemonnier held out his tin mug and Jonah poured in the last of their coffee. "Mr. Preston," the old man whispered, "I said the town hadn't told the army or you anythin' because it feared what Paton'd do. You see, we've tasted his terrorizin' from time to time—"

"But even Paton wouldn't ride right into Alkali Flat, surely!" Shane ventured.

"No, but he'd hang around on the trails outside of town, and it wouldn't be safe to ride out visitin' or come in for supplies," Lemonnier told them. "If Paton decided on reprisals, then no one would be safe beyond town limits, and our friends and relations on lonely settlements would be as good as in their graves."

"But you came out here and talked," Shane said.

Lemonnier sipped his coffee, then said, "You know, Mr. Preston, when them soldier-boys came to town askin' their questions, I nearly stepped out and talked—but somehow I held back. Mebbe it was because I've never had much confidence in the army. After all, if the bluebellies were much good, jaspers like Paton would have been run down ages ago. But when you came to town—Shane Preston and Jonah Jones—I kinda figured you'd do the job if I told the truth."

Shane grinned. "Thanks for the vote of confidence."

"The town didn't let on, but of course, most of us have heard of you—and the stories men tell about you. If I'd have let on to the army, they'd have most likely ridden out there with flags flyin' and bugles blastin'—Paton would have seen 'em comin' almost from here! They wouldn't have caught Paton, but Alkali Flat would have been on the receivin' end of some purty nasty reprisals."

"I don't figure the army's quite that foolish," Shane opined.

"Mr. Preston," said Lemonnier, "find Paton!"

"Paton and those guns," Shane said. "That it?"

"The guns, yes—but most of all—get Paton! Find the bastard and kill him for me!" A nerve was jumping in Lemonnier's temple. "I want Paton dead!"

Shane drew on his cigarette. Ebram Lemonnier hadn't ridden out of town merely to perform some patriotic duty by informing on the gang which had stolen the army guns. He'd come here and risked his neck because he believed that Shane and Jonah could carry out what seemed to be beyond the army—the killing of Drew Paton.

"A lot of folks want Paton dead, old-timer," Shane said softly.

"But none of 'em as much as me!" Ebram Lemonnier grated. "You see, Mr. Preston—he murdered my son!"

The two drifters and the Mormon said nothing as Lemonnier glared at them in turn.

"Yes, he murdered my boy, all I had," Lemonnier recalled bitterly. "Laban joined him, Mr. Preston. He was a fool, and he did it against my wishes, but he rode with Paton! That's how I know their hide-out! I didn't hear it from some prospectors who happened to be right—I heard it first-hand, from my son. You see, from time to time he rode to see me, to find out how his wife and kid were."

"And then what happened?"

"I heard the story months later, from an eyewitness in Faro. Seems Paton and his bunch hit the bank there. A gunfight broke out as they rode clear, and Laban, my son, was wounded. A posse was gathered, but when the outlaws reached town limits, Paton must have decided a wounded man would slow him down

68

and he didn't want to leave Laban to get caught and mebbe talk—so—so he shot my boy in cold blood. It was murder, Mr. Preston!"

"And now you hate Paton's guts," Shane nodded. "Makes sense."

"I want him dead! I want him in hell!"

"Thanks for coming out here, Ebram," Shane said. "Now I reckon you ought to down that coffee and head for home. And leave Paton to us."

"You'll—you'll see him in hell?"

"We'll do our best, Ebram."

The old man drained his coffee-mug and shuffled towards his horse. He climbed into the saddle, and they watched him turn his horse and head silently into the night. For a long moment, Shane said nothing. He was thinking of his own loss, of a wife who now lay in her grave, of a man he called Scarface who was riding around living and breathing and enjoying life. And somehow, his own memory and his own hatred helped him sympathize with Ebram Lemonnier. Yes, he'd see Paton in hell, given an even break.

It was the loneliest place in the world.

Below the huge, curving pumice rim, the wilderness stretched into the heat haze—a graveyard of slab rocks, drifting sand and awesome buttes which thrust up towards the burning sun. Not one tree could be seen, not a plant, not even a patch of mesquite.

The three riders surveyed the scene, and Lassetter mopped the dusty sweat from his forehead. To his credit, the young Mormon hadn't complained, even when the searing heat had been at its height, and he'd managed to keep up with the others as well. At sunrise, Shane had toyed with the notion of forcing Lassetter to leave them, but finally he'd decided to allow the young man to come with them. After all, an extra gun might prove helpful, especially as Lassetter's religion wasn't a pacifist one. And now they'd armed him with a spare gun.

"How much further?" Lassetter asked at last.

"Reckon we'll make it by sundown," Shane said. "Right now, though, we'll rest the horses."

John dismounted wearily, leading his bay to the vague shadow cast by a pumice rock. Shane filled his Stetson with water from his canteen and allowed Snowfire to drink.

"You always been a member of that new-fangled sect?" the tall Texan wanted to know.

"Only for a year."

"And your folks?"

Lassetter's face clouded and he swallowed. "When I became a saint, as we say, my earthly folks disowned me," he said. "My pa once said that if I submitted to the Mormon baptism, then I would no longer be his son."

"Any regrets?" Shane asked.

For a moment, Lassetter said nothing. "I have a new family now—the saints of God."

"That wasn't what I asked you."

"Mr. Preston," Lassetter said, "last night, when you dropped off to sleep, I had a long talk with Mr. Jones. He happened to tell me about your mission in life. He mentioned how you changed from a rancher into a drifter with a gun, all because of something terrible which happened to you. Have you any regrets, Mr. Preston?"

Shane could see that John was evading the question.

"You need to water your horse."

"Of course."

Shane walked over to where Jonah sat. The oldster was perched on the edge of the rim, his gnarled fingers building a cigarette.

"Damn strange coot, ain't he?" Jonah Jones remarked.

"He's different, Jonah," Shane said calmly. "That's why folks tried to hang him. But I'll grant one thing about him—he's got guts. By the way, did you realize we're being watched?"

"Noticed it since about noon," Jonah replied. "Figured you must know, but didn't want to alarm our Mormon friend."

"Might be nothing to get concerned about," Shane said, taking a drink from his canteen. "There's only one of them."

"He's Apache," Jonah stated, "and he's followin' us."

"Could be some buck with nothing to do," Shane said. "Whatever he's up to, there's nothing we can do about it right now. If we approach him, he's liable to ride off so we won't be any the wiser, and if we fire a warning shot over his head, it'll attract any of his friends who might be around."

"So we just keep ridin'?" Jonah mumbled around his drooping cigarette.

"Until he makes any fool move, that's all we can do."

"I seem to recall Tom Cannell mentioned Red Knife. Mebbe this buck's part of the renegade's bunch."

"In which case, we don't want to tangle with him— unless we're forced to. Our mission is to fetch back those guns, not to fight the army's Indian war."

"All the same," Jonah grunted, "he gives me the damn creeps, just sittin' up there watchin' us!"

"There's nothing we can do—yet," Shane said finally.

They smoked their cigarettes, and then Shane crossed back to John Lassetter. "Time to move," he said.

The scars on Old Wolf's face were the scars of time, for although the lean Apache rode with the younger men and from a distance could pass for a warrior half his years, he knew that his days were numbered. Like the days of the race he represented. Years ago, sitting here, he'd seen the trail made by his people as they trekked across the wilderness to better hunting grounds. All over this desert, he'd seen Apaches either moving or building lodges in readiness for winter. Then, even buffalo and other game ventured this far south. But now, only the drifting sand marked the mass graveyard of his people. They had fought the white intruders, attacked their wagon-trains, razed their settlements, but still the tide had flowed west. And in the end, this white tide had flooded over the land, until now only a few of his race remained. Some of these few had surrendered and the soldiers had herded them into reservations like cattle, but others had stayed on to fight, and to die. Old Wolf was one of those who would die—but die free.

Right now, his inscrutable, slitted eyes were fixed on the three riders below him. He'd ridden his pinto to the rim they'd descended from, and now he watched them as they picked their way towards the lonesome butte that shadowed the trail his father had once taken before this land was defiled. Old Wolf knew not who these intruders were. He only knew they were white men.

He waited until they were past the butte, then finally he turned his pinto pony. Red Knife would want to know of these men. Silently, like a shadow, the Apache moved off the rim.

SIX

THE GHOST TOWN

Sundown bathed the town of the dead, and the cold desert wind which had sprung up in the gray dusk whispered through the hushed, sand-silted streets and down the deserted alleys. It wasn't so very long ago that travelers coming down from this ridge would have seen a town lit with a hundred lamps and heard wild music coming from the saloons, but now Dry Creek was like a cemetery.

Lassetter shivered as a distant sound came to them—the banging of a shutter in the rising wind.

Shane's eyes rose to the battered sign.

TOWN OF DRY CREEK
Don't Forget To Call In At The French Lady Saloon

*

"Seems the proprietor had influence," Jonah Jones remarked. "An advertisement on the town sign!"

Shane looked beyond the sign to where Dry Creek stood as a silent monument to gold and greed. Some of the shacks on the outskirts had been so hastily erected that many of them lay in ruins under the silt. Further towards the town center, the streets of saloons and trading stores had withstood the passage of time and the elements, wrecked though they were.

"Paton's bunch could be holed up in any one of those buildings," Shane mused. "Reckon this is as far as we can go on horseback."

The tall drifter's boots crunched the dust, and he left Snowfire to the shadow of a boulder.

"Forgetting about angels and visitations and such-like," Shane murmured to Lassetter, "if you want to back out, you can stay here with the horses."

"I'm coming with you," the Mormon told his rescuers.

"See the old chapel?" Shane pointed out the only adobe building in town. "We'll make for there."

The trio began to edge forward, crossing the last tract of land to town limits. The chill wind moaned around them, whipping up sand around their feet. No one spoke as they ran past three dilapidated old shacks bordering the bone-dry creek bed which lent the town its name. They jumped down onto the creek bed. Two gecko lizards scampered away into the first clump of

75

bluestem grass Shane had seen for miles. Swiftly, the three men climbed the opposite bank and ran towards the old mission chapel. Shane dodged onto the porch. The door to the church was open, and the rows of pews were still there, just as they must have been at the last service of worship. Jonah and Lassetter joined him. The Mormon was carrying Shane's rifle.

"Shane!" Jonah whispered from the porch front.

The tall Texan stepped to his sidekick.

"A lamp," Jonah said, keeping his voice low. "Jest been lit down-street."

"'Looks promisin'."

"In one of the saloons, too," Jonah stated.

"'The French Lady'." Shane identified the liquor house. "Reckon we might do like the advertisement suggests—call in at the French Lady. Only, Jonah, you can mosey around the back way."

"What about me?" John Lassetter seemed eager, but his face was twitching.

"You come with me," Shane said.

"Sure." The Mormon was trembling. "And don't worry, friends, the lord is protecting us!"

It sounded like Lassetter was trying to reassure himself.

Jonah shuffled off across the street. Shane watched his sidekick reach an upturned water trough and run down a side alley to reach the rear of the French Lady.

"Ready, John?"

The Mormon gulped. "Yes."

Shane inched out from the porch, and with his eyes fixed on the slant of light splashing from the French Lady's window, he padded through the dust of the street. Lassetter, clutching his rifle like grim death, loped along beside him. The sound of drunken laughter floated to them on the wind, and Lassetter's face went a shade paler. Bottles littered the street near the saloon front. Shane halted at the corner of the saloon, and motioning John to remain there, the Texan edged slowly along the sandy board-walk. Another guffaw came from inside the saloon.

He made it to the corner of the window. Inch by inch, he moved his head so he could see inside. He had to brush dust away so he could see into the room. He peered through at the shadowy, cobweb-hung saloon. The garish place was a stark mockery of its former finery. The poker tables had been smashed to feed the open front of the wood stove. Only the bar-counter remained, and one man was lying full length on its top. Behind him, the picture of a nude female scribbled over with obscenities, maintained a silent vigil.

Shane made out four men, one of whom he recognized as Drew Paton. The group was sprawled on the stairs which led up to the balcony. Paton was drinking from a bottle and at least one other outlaw was dead drunk. Shane looked beyond the gang. A stack of crates lined the far wall. He could distinguish army markings. The Beals rifles!

"John," Shane whispered, "we're paying our friends a visit—right through the batwings. When it comes to gunfire, just drop where you are and keep on blasting like hell. Okay?"

"I'm ready," Lassetter assured him.

Shane crept to the batwings.

Still blissfully unaware of any danger, the out-laws continued their drinking and yahooing. Shane thumbed back the hammer of his gun, and even the sound of the hollow click passed unheard by those inside. The drifter shoved open the batwings and Moke's bronze face was a mask of shock as he was the first man to turn his head.

"Reach!" Shane's brittle command was like a whip crack. "I'll kill the first man to slap leather!"

"You bet!" John Lassetter jumped in beside Shane, his rifle leveled in his shaking hands. "All of you—reach!"

For a long moment, the four outlaws on the stairs simply stared in sheer disbelief at the two men. Vinton, prostrate on the bar, reared upright as if he'd been stung.

"Who in hell's name—?" Ringo spluttered.

"I'll tell you who he is," Drew Paton croaked, slowly raising his hands and standing up. "Shane Preston—do-gooder, drifter, you name it. I seem to remember runnin' into the bastard—where was it now?"

"Secundo," Shane reminded him dryly, "where you were jailed for rustling beeves."

"Mavericks," Paton corrected him.

"The rest of you—paws high!" It was Jonah in the rear doorway, his six-gun poised.

"Mr. Jonah Jones!" Paton said sarcastically.

The others raised their hands, glancing in bewilderment at their leader, amazed at his apparently easy surrender.

"Now, Preston," said Paton, "let me guess. You've come for the guns, huh?"

"The guns and you," Shane stated, stepping right into the saloon and leaving Lassetter at the batwings. "Looks like we've found both."

"Guess you've come on a wasted journey, Preston," the outlaw leader mocked him. "The rifles are here, sure enough, but you'll never get them back to where you figure on takin' them."

"You gonna try to stop us?" Jonah demanded.

"Not us, Jones," Paton laughed mirthlessly. "Someone's on his way to collect those rifles, and that someone would be hoppin' mad if they weren't here. In fact, Preston and Jones, he'd be so damn mad he'd chase after you and stake you out over an anthill."

"Mantez?" Shane asked.

Paton frowned. "How in hell do you know that?"

"Let's say someone else figured it out, Paton," Shane said, facing up to the outlaw boss. "Mantez is the only outlaw with the money to buy those rifles and the men to use them."

"Well, now," Paton complimented him, "that's right smart, Preston. Absolutely dead right, in fact. And Mantez is on his way to pick up the consignment and hand over the money for it. In fact, he's due tonight—or sunrise at the latest!"

"Which means we'll have to move," Shane nodded.

"Which means you better quit talkin' like a god-damn fool!" Drew Paton snapped at him. "Even if you leave now with these rifles, Mantez and his fifty men— yeah, fifty, Preston—would soon track you down and kill you. He certainly wouldn't let three loco fools like you just ride off with his guns. Now take my advice, all of you! Get!"

"Jonah," Shane said softly, "relieve these boys of their hardware."

"Don't be crazy!" the outlaw leader screeched. "You're committin' suicide! Hell, you'll be buzzard-bait!"

"Jonah—their hardware," Shane repeated.

Paton's face was contorted. He'd deliberately sur-rendered without a bleat because he'd been sure that the drifters would baulk at the notion of a showdown with Pedro Mantez. It seemed he'd miscalculated. Jonah shuffled towards them, filled with menace.

"Take them!" Drew Paton yelled.

The outlaw leader dropped his hand downwards, but only the half-liquored Vinton dared to follow his example. The others stood there as if frozen.

Shane's gun boomed first in the echoing saloon, and even as Drew Paton tried to drag his six-shooter from its holster, the slug struck home with a sickening thud. Paton tottered backwards, coughing blood, while Vinton angled around, suddenly cold sober as he gripped his gun. Jonah's gun hammer fell. The oldster's six-gun was alive and belching and Vinton folded as the bullet burned like a torch between his ribs.

Drew Paton was leaning back against the wall, blood gushing through his dirt-streaked shirt. The gun hung limply from his fingers.

"Reckon that slug was for Ebram Lemmonier," Shane said.

Then Paton crumpled and crashed dead to the floor. Jonah walked amongst the sullen outlaws, lifting guns from holsters and sticking them in his belt.

"Where's the gun-wagon?" Shane demanded.

"Out back," Jonah supplied. "Passed it on my way to the door."

"All right," Shane motioned to the three remaining outlaws with his six-gun, "load the gun crates into the wagon. We leave for Fort Dumas in ten minutes."

"You're—you're loco!" Ringo whispered. "Mantez and his men will kill you—and probably us, too, for helping you. Don't you realize? Mantez has fifty men! It's too far to the fort for you to outride them. They're bound to catch up!"

"Load the wagon," Shane snapped. He turned to the trembling John Lassetter. "Help Jonah guard them. I'll hitch their horses to the wagon."

Lassetter sprang forward to join Jonah. The Mormon jabbed his rifle muzzle into Ringo's stomach.

"You heard Mr. Preston!" Lassetter snapped. "He wants those guns in the wagon!"

And beside him, Jonah Jones grinned in his beard.

The cavalcade left a trail of churned-up sand under the rising moon and a single lamp was left burning in the French Lady Saloon. Shane rode ahead of the others, picking his way due south, heading towards the stage-trail, which would bring them within the shadows of Fort Dumas. Behind him, the wagon was being driven by John Lassetter, who bounced around on the front seat and flicked his whip over the team of horses. Stacked under the canvas were the Beals rifles. Jonah brought up the rear with the three outlaw prisoners, their wrists lashed together in front of them, strung together on a lead-rope.

Shane set a steady pace, mounting the long sand ridges and plunging down into the desert valleys, and soon the lone lamplight was swallowed up in the darkness as Dry Creek receded behind them.

For fully three hours the night travelers pushed southwards. Relentlessly, Shane pressed on, even when some of the horses began to stumble, and it wasn't until close to midnight that he raised his hand for a halt.

"How much longer to the stage-trail?" Lassetter asked, downing some water from the wagon-cask.

"Reckon we'll make it by mid-morning," the tall Texan predicted. "After that, it's an hour to the way-station where we'll rest up, then half a day to Fort Dumas."

Lassetter grinned. "You know, I was wondering."

"Yeah?"

"By now I ought to have been on that wagon-train for Salt Lake City, and here I am, helping you fellers escort these guns back to the fort. Wonder where my brother-saints on that wagon-train are now!"

"For all we know, they could be mighty close," Shane said. "Wagon-trains don't exactly move fast, and you probably only just missed your folks."

"Anyhow," the Mormon smiled, "I'm glad I missed them. You two men aren't exactly saints. I mean, you smoke, drink alcohol and coffee, and sometimes Mr. Jones uses some—well, terrible language which isn't very godly—but I wouldn't have missed this experience for anything. At least, when I finally reach Salt Lake City and the saints, I'll have a story to tell!"

"The story's not over yet," Shane warned. "It's a long trail to Fort Dumas, and Mantez must want these rifles real bad."

"Mantez …" John Lassetter mused. "I've heard such terrible stories about him. Can he really be that evil?"

"He's a bad one, sure enough," Shane Preston assured him. "Never met up with him, but I know him by reputation. Once, he was a sheriff south of the border."

"Mantez a lawman!"

"Sheriff of a little Mexican village," Shane said, recalling the story. "Turned out to be a back-shooting sheriff who became a bandido, an outlaw. But he became a bandido with a difference. He had a hatred for Americans. I know a treaty's been signed, recognizing the independence of Texas from Mexico, but Mantez is one greaser who doesn't recognize it. Probably figures he's still fighting at the Alamo. Anyhow, he raids north of the border, raping, killing and looting in a kind of personal crusade against Texans."

"And the army's never been able to stop him?"

"How do you catch an outfit which strikes and then vanishes into the desert? Even when the army has gotten onto his trail, he's sneaked south of the border and lost his pursuers in the Cruz Mountains."

"And this Mantez might be on our trail?" Lassetter shivered suddenly.

"Not might be—will be, thanks to Paton and his murderin' crew."

"What kind of Americans can they be—selling guns to men like Mantez?" The Mormon shook his head in disbelief.

BANDIDO!

"The worst kind," Shane said. "In actual fact, Mantez probably hates their guts, too. He'll only be dealing with any Americans because it suits him, and a deal for a hundred new rifles would suit him just fine."

"Shane!" Jonah's croaking voice rang out from beside the wagon. "The ridge!"

The tall drifter angled around, his keen eyes immediately picking out what Jonah had spotted. Some dozen riders were lining the moonlit ridge, silent watchers dominating the desert below.

"Fires of hell!" The outlaw Davenish drew in his breath sharply. "Damn Apaches! Now we're done for!"

Shane went over to his sidekick, not taking his eyes off the ridge. The dark riders were like statues, men and ponies silhouetted against the jeweled sky.

"That blasted buck must have gone and fetched his pards," Jonah muttered.

"Leave the guns here," Ringo suggested hoarsely. "Let those Indians come down here and search the wagon while we ride like hell outa here! Once they get their paws on the repeaters they'll be so moonstruck they'll soon forget about us!"

"And those rifles will give them the means to butcher innocent settlers all along the frontier," Shane said grimly. "Handing the guns to the Apaches would be as big a crime as letting them go to Mantez."

"To hell with these innocent settlers of yours!" Ringo snarled. "And anyway, what choice do we have? That goddamn gun wagon will slow us down! Them painted devils will catch up with us and scalp us all!"

"Ain't it against the Indian religion for them to fight at night?" Jonah submitted hopefully.

"I've heard that," Shane Preston agreed, "but in case there are some heretics amongst them, I wouldn't bet more than a dime on it."

"Preston," Davenish wailed, "you—you can't leave us tied up like this with those butchers out there! Hell, you are a white man!"

Shane was thoughtful for a moment. He glanced at the gun wagon with its load of weapons which could set the frontier ablaze if it fell into the wrong hands, then back at the prisoners. These three men were being taken back for trial, and each one of them knew the outcome—a swift hanging.

"I'm tempted to give you three skunks a fighting chance," Shane murmured, "though God knows you don't deserve one. Jonah—cut them loose."

The oldster shrugged as he sliced through their rawhide ropes. The outlaws rubbed their wrists with their hands, over and over.

"Climb down from your horses," Shane ordered.

The three outlaws obeyed.

"What now?" Ringo growled.

"You know," Shane said, looking hard at the stubble-faced trio, "I'm going to give you three low-down skunks the chance to do something decent for once, something for other folks. Ringo said he didn't give a damn about innocent settlers. Well, I figure that's the wrong attitude, and I'm about to give you hombres the chance to change it."

"What the hell are you gettin' at, Preston?" Davenish demanded.

"If those Indians get their hands on these guns, a lot of decent settlers will suffer. You're going to help make sure that doesn't happen."

"Huh?" Ringo screwed up his face, mystified.

"What d'you mean?" Moke grunted.

"You three boys are going to be decoys," Shane told them. "You'll be right here, on the desert sand, without horses—just in case you decide to be unpatriotic and ride out leaving the army guns to the enemy. You'll have guns, of course, and cartridges. Reckon that the Indians won't be able to resist an attack, and in the meantime, we'll be taking those Beals rifles well out of their reach. Could be we'll have just enough time to ride clear of this bunch. As for you, if you die, you'll die as heroes, not the lousy gun-running outlaws you really are. But if you live, well, I reckon you'll have earned your freedom."

"What sorta chance have we got of that happening?" Davenish demanded.

"Better than your chance with the hangman," Shane reminded him bluntly. "At least I'm going to give you guns."

"Mebbe those redskins will leave us alone and just chase after the gun-wagon," Ringo whispered to his white-faced companions.

"Maybe." Shane had heard the whisper from the optimistic Ringo. "But most unlikely, Ringo. After all, the Indians have no way of knowing what's in that gun-wagon, and I reckon the three of you down here will be too much of a temptation for them to pass up."

The drifter glanced up at the line of Indians. Not one of them had moved on the dark ridge.

"Tie their horses to the wagon," Shane told Jonah.

They waited until the oldster had completed this chore. Then Shane picked up the three guns that the outlaws had been relieved of back in the French Lady and tossed them in the sand. Jonah added some cartridges to the pile.

"Get moving!" Shane yelled to the Mormon.

John Lassetter lashed the team into a jolting start, and the wagon creaked away. The two drifters hastily mounted up, leaving Ringo and the other outlaws to stare at the guns on the sand.

"It's your chance to do something decent," Shane called back to them, urging Snowfire after the wagon.

"Go to hell!" Davenish screeched, swooping up his six-gun and fumbling with cartridges. The outlaw whipped the gun up level, aiming at Shane's retreating back. Ringo's restraining hand found Davenish's wrist.

"I hate the bastard, too," Ringo told him. "But we can't take all three of 'em! And we'll need every slug for those Indians!"

Slowly, Davenish lowered his gun-hand. Beads of sweat stood out like drops of rain on his forehead.

"And despite what I said to Preston," Ringo added, "I would rather this than a hangman's noose."

They looked around at the receding gun-wagon. Lassetter was whipping the horses with frenzied vigor, and the two Texans were riding right alongside him, adding their yells to his lash in order to urge the team into an even greater speed.

Davenish groaned. "The Apaches—look!"

"They're comin' down." Ringo swallowed. "Seems like the story about their religion not permittin' war at night ain't strictly true. Well, let's give the devils a hot reception. Hey ... wait on!"

Ringo grabbed hold of Moke's arm.

"What is it, Ringo?" Moke grunted, checking his gun.

"Why, of course! Moke, you're one of 'em. I mean, you're a 'breed—part-Apache."

"Which means they'll torture me if I'm taken alive," Moke told him grimly. "They hate men like me, part-white, part-Indian, belonging to neither race."

"But you can speak their lingo!" the other insisted.

"Talk to them," Davenish croaked, catching on to Ringo's thoughts. "Walk out and talk. Tell them about those guns. Tell them about the Beals rifles that they could miss out on if they waste time on us."

"They—they wouldn't listen to me," Moke protested.

"Listen, Moke," Ringo gritted, "they might hate your damn guts, but they sure want those guns. Go talk!"

The Indians were filing down from the ridge, melting from shadow to shadow like ghosts. Davenish scrambled into a shallow gulch and Ringo sprawled down beside him. Only Moke was standing, watching, waiting as the wind began to rise to an eerie moan.

By now the wagon had vanished.

"Call out to 'em, Moke," Davenish urged him.

The 'breed took several paces away from the gulch. The wind whipped dust around him as he stumbled to a halt, then cupped his lips with his hands.

"We want to talk!" Moke's guttural voice pronounced the words in the Apache tongue. "We are your friends, and we want to talk about you getting a hundred rifles!"

But his only answer was the steady whine of the desert wind. A cloud raced across the moon, plunging the wilderness into inky blackness. One by one the stars seemed to be doused by an unseen hand, and Moke shivered as he stood there alone. He knew they were out there—somewhere. By now, they would have all reached the foot of the ridge, and they'd be silently encircling the gulch.

"Apache friends!" Moke's desperate voice rang out in the darkness. "We must talk about you getting those rifles!"

Right then, the scudding clouds passed on, and a sudden slant of moonlight splashed over the desert, fingering the sand and the rocks in a split moment of time. In one terrible second, the moonlight showed the three outlaws the dark circle of death which surrounded them. The Apaches had moved down like silent ghosts and now they sat on their pinto ponies surveying their prey.

"Apache friends! My brothers! Listen to me!"

A lance sung through the night air and plunged into Moke's chest. The half-breed staggered forward, pleading with them, groping for his gun. Two rifles were raised, old army carbines stolen from dead soldiers, and they thundered simultaneously. Moke pitched backwards, dead before he hit the sand.

"God!" Davenish whispered. "They didn't even give him a chance to talk!"

"They probably figured he was just stallin'," Ringo said. "And mebbe he was right. He was a 'breed, so they hated his guts and decided to kill him regardless."

"Why—why don't they come and git us?" Davenish said, out of a dry mouth. His fingers were slippery on his gun. "Why do they just sit around like a lot of goddamn buzzards?"

"They'll come soon enough," Ringo told him. His tone was that of a gambler who knows when the throw is lost.

It was almost as if they had heard Ringo's statement. Indians began slipping from their ponies, brandishing their carbines as they prepared to rush the outlaws in the gulch. Ringo's six-gun roared and a brave spun around with a slug in his belly. Suddenly, the Apaches surged in on the gulch. The two outlaws pumped shot after shot at them. Three Indians crashed to the sand. Another ran, limping, away, but the others came on like a dark, wild tide. Their ancient carbines were booming now. Ringo caught a bullet high in the shoulder and he sank moaning over his smoking gun. With blood spilling down his chest to his belt, he lifted his head. A fierce, triumphant Indian loomed over him. Ringo shot half his face away at point blank range, and the Indian dropped. Behind him, Davenish was frantically reloading. Still the savages charged them. Ringo's gun roared at two oncoming redskins but even as one folded, his carbine bucked. There was a dull, terrible thud and Ringo was pitched onto his back, his staring eyes looking sightlessly up at the moon. Panic-stricken, Davenish clambered out of the gulch. One of the riderless Indian ponies was close to their position and, desperately, the outlaw plunged after the wiry little horse. He weaved between two dodging Apaches, then clawed his way onto the pony's back. A single shot blasted out. Davenish felt pain like an agonizing knife in his spine. He slid from the pony's back, helpless, unable to move. And then the shadows stood around him—fierce desert men with fire burning in their eyes. Davenish was pleading, swearing, praying, all in the same breath as one of the Indians took a long knife from his sheath.

"Now—you talk!" the Apache with the knife said in faltering English. "Coyote half-breed spoke of guns."

Wracked with agony, Davenish groped up to cling to the man's brawny arm. Here was a reservation-bred Indian, one who understood his language! Like a drowning man grasping at a tiny straw, Davenish fastened his fingers into the Apache brave's flesh.

"Don't kill me!" Davenish whimpered. "I'll talk—yes—I'll tell you everything you want to know—only spare me, for the love of God!"

"Our hatred for the 'breed made us too hasty with lance and gun," the Indian stated. "But he spoke of guns."

"In the wagon!" Davenish blurted out. "A hundred guns! Enough and more for all of you. And they're yours if you catch that wagon! Think of what you—you can do with them. You—you could rule the desert with those guns—all latest Beals repeater rifles! Do you savvy what I'm saying?"

"I savvy." The Apache turned to the others and repeated Davenish's statement to them in his own tongue.

"You—you won't kill me, will you?" Davenish blubbered like a frightened child.

Very slowly and deliberately, the Indian prised Davenish's fingers from his arm.

"I—I told you what you wanted to know! I'm your friend, don't you see? The Apaches' friend. Now, just ride off and—and leave me here. I'll sorta take my chances—"

The knife glimmered in the moonlight. Then the blade plunged down and ripped into Davenish's heart.

SEVEN

THE DEATH RIDERS

The smoke was rising leisurely, floating into the azure sky from the long ridge.

Shane, riding ahead of the gun-wagon on the rutted stage trail, spotted the blue-gray signals first. The tall man raised his hand, and Jonah spurred old Tessie alongside of him as he came to a halt.

"Can you read 'em?" Jonah asked anxiously.

"Reckon it's some sort of summons to a powwow," Shane Preston predicted. "Maybe Apaches calling for reinforcements."

"Bet it's that bunch from last night!" Jonah growled. "They must have ridden ahead of us, and now they're callin' on their blood-brothers to help them attack us on the trail."

Shane squinted at the smoke. "Nope, I don't figure it's the same bunch, Jonah."

"Huh! You mean there's more than one bunch of the devils around here?"

"The boys on that ridge last night were just a scouting party. There's more than a score of Apaches along the trail. I've been noticing Indian signs ever since we reached it. The bunch that passed this way recently is double that number, maybe more."

"And this outfit could have us in mind!" Jonah looked up at the smoke signals.

"Maybe. We can't know for sure. According to my calculations, we're not far from that way-station I saw on Tom Cannell's map. Could well be the other side of the ridge. Indians gettin' as close as that to a white man's way-station is mighty ominous."

"And where does that leave us?" Jonah asked.

"With a wagon-load of rifles those Indians must not lay their hands on," Shane said grimly. "And close to a way-station where some white folks might just be in real trouble."

"So what happens now?"

"Reckon we head for the way-station," Shane said. "And take it from there."

John Lassetter had glimpsed the signals too, and he was as agitated as a bullfrog on a hot griddle-iron.

Shane wheeled Snowfire to the wagon. "John, we're about to move out of here as fast as we can. If those red varmints haven't seen us yet, they soon will—but regardless of what happens, we just keep going till we hit the way-station that can't be too far ahead."

The Mormon nodded, picking up his long whip.

"Shane!" Jonah summoned him. "Reckon them braves have spotted us! The ridge is lousy with 'em."

"Okay, John—get the horses moving!" Shane commanded.

The Mormon's whip cracked over the team, and the horses surged forward. To the north of the trail, painted riders lunged down the dusty slopes. A distant carbine boomed. Then two more guns thundered, but the distance was too great for effectual shooting. The wagon was swaying along like a galleon before the wind, with Shane and Jonah right alongside. The wheels fairly sang over the hard ground. John yelled his lungs out and the whip cracked out time and time again. For a fleeting moment, it looked as if wagon and Apaches would surely meet, but Lassetter gained an extra ounce of effort from the team and the gun-wagon rumbled past the foot of the ridge and headed around a towering butte. The Apaches milled together on the trail, gesticulating with their carbines, screaming themselves hoarse. On plunged the wagon, sliding around on the trail as it turned down into a long, shallow valley. Right ahead was the way-station. Two Apaches stood like sentinels on a dusty rise overlooking the way-station, and when they saw the billowing dust and the rumbling wagon, they leveled their carbines.

Shane's six-shooter belched first. The foremost Indian pitched from his pinto like a falling tree. The other Apache fired wildly and the slug ripped through the canvas behind Lassetter. The Indian raised his gun again, but Jonah's six-gun spat death from his hip and the painted brave crashed to the ground. Careering in a pall of dust, the wagon continued at full speed to the way-station, and suddenly the front door was thrust open and a rifle protruded. A thick-set man lumbered onto the porch, emptying his gun into the bunch of Apaches who were riding in the wake of the wagon. The Indians veered off at a tangent, melting into the valley.

Shane glanced over to the wagon. Lassetter had jammed on the brake-lever and pulled the team to a shuddering halt right alongside a stagecoach, and now the Mormon was clambering down. The tall drifter slipped from his saddle, joining the burly man on the porch.

"Shane Preston," he announced curtly and the man nodded.

"Seen your picture in more than one newspaper over the past year. I'm Leif Portland—this is my place."

Shane shook hands then scanned the valley where the dust was slowly settling.

"Thanks for your help," Shane said.

"Those damn Apaches have been around here most of the day—Red Knife's bunch of killers. They chased the stage in here and they've had us under siege ever since."

"The stage passengers here too?" Shane demanded. The last visible Indian was riding his pony up the distant ridge.

"Yeah," nodded Portland. "And a damn odd outfit they are, too. Some of them ran into the way-station like spooked hens, so I just handed them all guns and told them to start shootin' if they wanted to stay alive."

"How'd it work?"

"Passable. We've had two big attacks, and managed to fight 'em off both times. I've stationed someone at every door and window."

Shane nodded. "Meet my saddle pard—Jonah Jones."

"Howdy." Then Portland frowned at the Mormon. "Didn't figure there were three of you."

"John Lassetter's with us for a while," Shane said.

"Pleased to meet up with you, Lassetter. Reckon you all might as well come inside."

"First of all, there are some crates we must bring in."

"Crates?"

"Full of Beals rifles," Shane explained. "The consignment stolen from the army escort a short while ago. We're taking them back to Fort Dumas and it could be a mite tempting to the Indians if they were left outside."

"Hell, yes!" Portland agreed.

The front door opened, and the blocky figure of ex-sheriff Woode stood there.

"I've been listenin'," Judd Woode admitted. "Want a hand with those gun-crates?"

The five men went to the wagon, and soon the heavy crates were being shuttled across the porch and through the front door. The other passengers began to gather in the dining room as the crates were stacked along the wall. Just before the last crate was carried in, the gambler van Elnin, volunteered his services and assisted in shouldering the final load of guns. All this time, Abel Dancer, the deserter, watched from a table in the corner.

The stage-driver, Matt Starrett, trudged in from the kitchen and whistled when he saw the crates.

"Sufferin' snakes! What those Apaches wouldn't give to get their lousy paws on these!" he exclaimed.

Lorn van Elnin gave him an odd look.

"I reckon everyone ought to get back to his post," suggested Portland. Everyone except Dancer moved away. "You too, Dancer."

The deserter rose painfully from his chair. There was a hard smile on his face, but nevertheless he shuffled obediently to a side window and checked the carbine he had been given.

"If you folks are hungry," said Portland, "I'll get my daughter to rustle up some chow."

"And drink," Jonah added quickly. "Coffee for two. Count John out—coffee's against his religion."

"Huh?" Portland frowned.

"Sarsaparilla for my friend." Shane clapped Lassetter on the shoulder.

"Sure, sure," Leif Portland looked amazed. He went down the passage, and the travelers sat down. Then a buxom blonde woman wearing an apron over her skirt came in. She had a beaming smile, and when she spoke, her voice boomed like a man's.

"I can hardly say welcome to our way-station, gentlemen," she thundered. "Not with whoopin' Apaches ringing the valley. My name's Cassie Portland—Leif's wife."

"Ma'am," Jonah smiled, doffing his Stetson.

The woman went on, "And to think this is the first time I've even seen a confounded Indian since we came to take over this way-station!"

She smoothed down her hair, catching Jonah's wink. Plump women had always been Jonah's specialty, but right now Shane didn't want any discord in the way-station so he aimed a hefty kick at his partner's shins under the table.

"Ow!" yipped Jonah.

"Anything wrong, Mr. Jones?" Cassie asked, concerned.

"Pesky sandbug bit me!" Jonah grimaced at Shane.

Five minutes later, the door to the passage swung open and a slim, willowy girl walked through. She had the same looks as Leif and Cassie Portland, but unaccountably her build was the very opposite.

"My daughter, Miriam," Cassie said with pride.

Shane appraised her frankly. She was much taller than her mother, fine-boned, with an oval face fringed by corn-gold hair that cascaded to her slender shoulders. Miriam would be in her twenties, Shane judged, and as he looked at her, he saw the firm buds of her breasts deliciously moving as she approached their table.

"I've brought your drinks," she told them.

"Miriam," John Lassetter mused. "A truly lovely Biblical name."

She smiled gently at the compliment, and Shane noted that the Mormon had already made an impression. Now he realized how Alkali Flat's men had feared for their womenfolk with him around.

"Two cups of coffee," she said, "and one sarsaparilla."

"I'm one of the saints," Lassetter explained to her.

"The saints?"

"He's a Mormon, ma'am," Shane said bluntly.

"Oh." Her eyes were wide. "I'll fetch your food presently." She went out again.

Lassetter scowled. "What did you say it like that for?"

"I told her the truth," Shane said, stirring his coffee.

"But there are different ways of telling the truth, Mr. Preston," the Mormon argued. "You could have been more—shall we say—subtle."

"Listen to me, John. All our lives are at stake here, and I can't risk any quarrels. That means no preaching your beliefs, specially to impressionable young females. Savvy?"

"I savvy," Lassetter agreed grumpily.

A tall lean figure edged through the passage door. Lorn van Elnin's fine suit had long since been marred by dust, and even his hair had alkali in it. "Mr. Preston?" he said.

"That's me."

"I have a suggestion, Mr. Preston." The gambler rubbed his hands together. "I thought you might like to hear it."

"Who are you?" Jonah growled.

"Lorn van Elnin, a gentleman of the tables," the gambler introduced himself. "I happen to be heading west with my wife, Binnie."

"And what's your suggestion?" Shane asked.

"Correct me if I'm wrong, Mr. Preston," he purred, "but it seems to me that our chances are slim. We're outnumbered by a savage horde who intend to kill each and every one of us …"

"Say, Preston!" Abel Dancer cut in from his post at the front window.

Shane leaped up, brushed past the gambler and joined the deserter who was pointing out.

"See what's happenin'? A small band of Indians just arrived on the scene and talked with Red

Knife—that's the big bastard with the yeller bandanna round his head."

"So?"

"So they keep pointing to their carbines and then down at the wagon. I might be reading something that ain't there, but it seems to me this new bunch is telling Red Knife that wagon carried guns. It's a chance Red Knife saw us carryin' in the crates, but from that distance, he couldn't have known what was in them—probably figured they were belongings from the wagon."

"I reckon you're reading it right," Shane agreed quietly. "Seems just about the whole damn tribe is gathering now. Those new boys have certainly brought in good tidings for them all."

"I don't suppose those outlaws talked?" Jonah suggested, coming to stand with Shane.

"One thing's for sure," growled Shane. "If Red Knife knows the rifles are here, he'll come—and soon."

"Which brings me to my suggestion," van Elnin said at his elbow.

Shane said sharply, "How come?"

"I suggest we make a deal with them."

"What kinda deal?" Jonah demanded.

"We want our freedom, our lives—they want the guns. Say we ride out and tell them about the cache, then bargain with them. Things have been made simpler for us. We don't even have to dicker. They must know about the guns. All we have to do now is make a simple deal. Our lives for the handing over of the consignment of guns. No bloodshed, no killing. Just a straight forward, peaceful deal."

"Hell! Hand guns over to Indians!" Dancer was aghast.

"Tinhorn," Shane said, choosing his words with care, "get back to your post before I put my fist in your big mouth!"

"Now see here—" the gambler blustered.

"You heard me!" Shane's fingers gripped the man's lapels.

"What will playing hero get you?" van Elnin sneered. "A stake-out over an anthill?"

"Your post!" snapped Shane.

Grumbling, the gambler ambled back down the passage.

"You know, I'm not over-sure there's any difference between him and those outlaws!" Shane Preston murmured.

Soup was brought in by Miriam, and the three newcomers gulped some down swiftly. They ate with their guns close at hand.

"You rotten coward!" Binnie van Elnin wept.

"Hush up!" her husband snapped, looking out of the rear window where he'd been posted.

"I heard it all," she said, wiping her eyes with the back of her hand. "Every vile word!"

"You shouldn't have listened to men's talk!" he accused her.

"Men?" She laughed scornfully. "You'll never be a man. A man works for a living—you've always trusted to luck and a little cheating. A man faces life, maybe death—you want to hand over those guns knowing the Indians would use them to butcher innocent settlers, even kids! All because you're scared!"

"Aren't you scared?" van Elnin asked suddenly.

She swallowed. "Maybe."

"Let me tell you something, Binnie," the gambler said hoarsely. "You married me because we're two of a kind, and when death faces you, you'll run—the same as me."

Binnie stared at him scornfully. "The biggest mistake of my life was when I married you, Lorn van Elnin!"

And with that, she swept from the room to resume her post at the parlor window. Just a few paces away, Matt Starrett was at the door to the backyard. The stage-driver stubbed his cigarette against the wall, his eyes focused on van Elnin's wife. Because of the Apache attack, he hadn't been able to carry on his flirtation with Binnie but right now things seemed to be quiet outside.

"Trouble with that husband of yours, ma'am?" the stage driver said, looking at her tear-streaked face.

"What do you do when you find out you've married a lowdown, cheating coward?" she asked bitterly.

"Never been in that predicament," he said banteringly. He came to stand right behind her, and Binnie could hear his heavy breathing. She'd been aware of his frank glances from the time she'd boarded the stage. At first, she'd felt flattered, now she was trembling. She started when his fingers clasped her shoulders and a little cry escaped her lips.

"Know what I'd do, ma'am?" Starrett murmured softly. "If I was a woman like you, a decent, purty woman, I'd be finding myself another man—a real man, that is."

She closed her eyes, acutely aware that his right hand had drifted over her shoulder. Normally, she would have protested at such a bold liberty being taken, or at least have brushed his hand aside, but suddenly she didn't care—maybe even welcomed his attentions.

"Mr. Starrett …" she breathed.

"Matt," he corrected her thickly.

She leaned back against him, her eyes shut tight. His fingers deftly unhooked the top three buttons of her dress while his mouth muzzled her hair. His hand was hard against her flesh—so different from the soft, smooth gambler's hands she'd known so long.

She opened her mouth to utter a token protest as that harsh, demanding hand slipped right inside her dress and cupped her breast. She gasped, half from pain, half from desire. Then she found herself being swung around and hot, quivering lips were clamped ruthlessly over her mouth. Binnie struggled, but as his passion mounted, she allowed herself to go limp in his arms. Starrett kissed her long and hard, and very slowly, as her stirring passion matched his own, Binnie wound her soft arms around his neck. They swayed together at the window, two silhouettes molded fiercely together as one.

Suddenly there was a shattering crash and glass fragments flew wildly around them both. Starrett jerked from the embrace, then stood motionless with his eyes filming over. As blood began to spill out of his mouth, the woman screamed hysterically. Matt Starrett seemed to sway, then plunged to the floor—an Apache lance buried to the barb in his side.

The desert sprang to deadly life as waves of Indians rose from the sand, racing towards the way-station on foot. Weeping, Binnie had the presence of mind to pick up her rifle. She knelt down below the sill, and as she poked her gun through the jagged glass, other guns thundered from the way-station. On came Red Knife's warriors, lean, bronzed men of the wilderness, charging in to destroy. Binnie remembered her girlhood days on the frontier. Her aim was steady as she fired. A tall sinuous buck climbing the corral fence was lifted from the wooden rails by the bullet's impact. He slumped to the ground, and two other Indians lunged past him. Binnie pumped three more slugs at the elusive bronze shadows, then dodged low as more glass was shattered in her face.

A fusillade of flying lead thudded into the way-station. Two more windows were shattered. The front door hung precariously on a single hinge. Still the human tide flowed on. In the front room, Dancer's cheek was nicked by a searing bullet and blood spurted down over his ripped tunic. One Indian clambered into the stage, and Shane shot half his head away. Two more padded along the front porch, and one painted face appeared at the window Dancer had been defending. An old carbine slithered over the sill. Jonah, crouched low behind a table, whipped up his gun and fired in a single deft movement. The bullet carved into the bridge of the Apache's nose and there was a hollow thud as his body hit the wooden boards of the porch.

Seconds later, the Indians melted back into the wilderness, and an eerie hush settled over the valley.

"Seems like you're running this show now, Preston," the gambler sneered as they answered his summons and gathered around him in the main room.

"This is my station, and I've asked Shane to take over," Leif Portland told him tersely.

"I might have been placed in charge," Shane said, "but I'm open to any suggestions—except the one you put up, van Elnin."

The gambler shrugged and reached for his cigar case.

"How do you see things?" the former lawman, Judd Woode asked the drifter.

"Those Indians probably know about the rifles, which means they'll keep on coming—and we haven't the numbers to hold out forever. We've one hope—someone to ride to Fort Dumas for help, and that would have to be done under cover of dark. I'm calling for a volunteer, preferably someone who knows the desert."

There was a long silence. Lorn van Elnin struck a match and lit his cigar as Shane ran his eyes over the group.

"A volunteer?" the gambler demanded. "A volunteer for what? Death at the hands of those red savages?"

"Someone to give the rest of us hope," Shane countered. "And more important than us—to give hope to others on this frontier. Reckon I've already spelled out what'll happen to a whole lot of settlers if the Apaches lay hands on those Beals guns."

Van Elnin puffed on his cigar. "Sounds right worthy! But if you ask me, my solution is the only good one, the only one that makes sense."

Shane ignored him. "The volunteer must know the desert back-trails because Red Knife's warriors will be watching the main trail. He'd also need to be slippery to sneak through even though it'll be dark."

Jonah grimaced. "Reckon I'll play the hero."

"You might be slippery, mister," Woode said, smiling at the oldster, "but you're like most of us here— you wouldn't know the back-trails."

"I'd have a damn good try at findin' them!" the whiskery one snorted. "Besides, I ain't exactly in knee britches now, you know, and if anything happens to me, it'll be just too bad."

Shane said quietly, "Not you, Jonah."

All this time, Abel Dancer had been sitting on the floor. Miriam had swabbed his face wound. It was not serious, but he had bled a lot. Now he stood up and leaned against the log wall.

"There's only one man who's been around this desert long enough to know the back-trails," Dancer said evenly. "Just one. I reckon Preston knows who that one is. That man mightn't be the best one to sneak past that ring of Indians, but if he could do it, he'd have no trouble makin' the fort."

"And who the heck are you suggesting?" van Elnin demanded.

Dancer looked hard at Shane Preston. "Me," the deserter said.

111

Judd Woode looked nonplussed, while Lianna gaped. Beside them, Binnie, still shocked by the memory of how Starrett had died, stared into the distance. Most of the others showed their bewilderment at Dancer's shock offer—all except Shane and van Elnin.

It was the gambler who broke the silence with a laugh of derision. It was followed by Shane's quiet, even voice:

"You're the man, soldier."

EIGHT

THE DARKNESS OF DEATH

It was a sullen sunset without a breath of wind. All was quiet.

"I've heard a lot about you, Shane," Miriam said as she brought him coffee where he stood close to the smashed window in the men's guest room. "But I never knew you were a gambler."

"What makes you think I am now?" He accepted the coffee with a nod of thanks.

"Abel Dancer," she said. "After all, he is a deserter."

"You know, Miriam," he said, sipping the coffee, "when I was a kid I used to sit at the table and listen to some of my pa's sayings. At the time, I listened with a smile to a few of the things he said. Now he's gone, I've come to realize that a lot of what he said was true."

"And he said something about deserters?" She was undecided whether to smile or frown.

"About cowards in general, ma'am," he said. "My pa believed that no man or woman was a complete coward. In fact, he said there's the makings of a hero in just about everyone, given the right situation to bring it out."

"It certainly wasn't brought out when Abel Dancer deserted his patrol and the Apaches attacked," she commented dubiously.

"Not then," he agreed.

"And how do you know he won't just ride out of the way-station, sneak past the Indians and make his escape?"

"He wouldn't head for the fort, that's for sure. He's been drummed out. I'm taking a chance that he wants to go back—for us. To prove something."

Miriam placed her hands on her hips. "You know something, Shane Preston? You're different from what I expected."

"How's that?"

"Well …" She sought for the right words. "Whenever folks mentioned Shane Preston they gave the impression you were a—well, a gunslinger, a man who hired out his gun for cash."

"That's my trade," Shane agreed. "From time to time I have to hire out. But only if it's for a good reason, a good cause."

"You need a stake while you hunt down Scarface?"

He looked at her sharply. "Old Whiskers has been blabbing!"

"Jonah Jones and I did have a little talk," she said. "You must have loved your wife very dearly, Shane."

"She meant everything to me," he said quietly.

"So much so that no other woman could ever take her place?" Miriam whispered.

Shane looked at her intently. "No one."

"I—I thought that might be the way it is," Miriam said regretfully.

"Thanks for the coffee," he said, handing her back the empty cup.

The girl left him at the window, and Shane looked out at the silent desert. And as the darkness came, so did the memories return.

"I'll be praying for you, even though you're not a baptized saint," John Lassetter told the ex-soldier.

"Thanks," Abel Dancer said wryly. He slid the loaded six-gun into his holster. "I'll need every prayer you can offer."

"Is the horse ready?" Shane asked.

"Right out back," Leif Portland said. "I've covered its hoofs with cloth, just like you said."

"The redskins have lit a fire," Jonah observed from the front window.

Shane went to join his sidekick. A crimson glow lit up the distant valley wall, illuminating the steep sides and craggy heights. The Indians had built their fire right at the base of the sandstone, and Shane could see dark figures moving in and out of the firelight.

"Shane," Abel Dancer said softly, finding him at the window. "When—when I volunteered, I never figured for one moment you'd actually accept me—because of what I am."

"You want to back out?" Jonah demanded.

"No," Dancer said quietly. There was a strange, haunted look in his eyes. "But I must warn you. What happened before might happen again. I have to say that before I ride."

"Last time you betrayed a platoon of soldiers," Shane said. "This time you'd be betraying hundreds of people on the frontier. Just think about that as you ride on out."

Like distant thunder came a deep throbbing from the Indian camp, incessant, nerve-tingling, and as she came to stand beside Shane, Miriam shivered. The drumming mounted. There were no war whoops, no yelling, just the rolling drums.

"Could make things easier for you, Abel," Shane said, leading him towards the back door. "With that infernal din, they'll be less likely to hear your horse."

It was an attempt at encouragement, and Dancer nodded. The deserter paused on the back porch, then swung into the saddle. One by one, the people filtered out to watch him ride off carrying their hopes, and maybe some of their fears. Dancer turned his face from them. The back that had been branded still ached, reminding him of that stark, ugly moment when the hot iron had been pressed to his flesh. That 'D' would never fade. It was with him forever. If he stripped off his shirt for any reason, everyone would know. Should he marry, his wife would know she was making love to a deserter. He shook off the thought, heading his horse slowly away from the way-station.

Just once he looked behind him. There were no lamps burning in Portland's way-station, and the entire building was wreathed in darkness. The drumming grew louder as Dancer moved further away from the way-station, and it almost seemed as if the huge campfire was a beacon for him. His horse gave out a soft whicker. Dancer swore at the unwelcome sound; and cold pin-pricks of sweat formed on his forehead. He had the feeling of being very much alone—yet not alone! Suddenly he was back in that canyon where his platoon had been trapped, and once again he saw himself riding to the narrow knife-edge pass in the pitch blackness. How lonely he'd felt! And how scared of death—like now! He tried to reason within himself, just as he'd tried back in that pass. Death was the lot of all men, himself included. Only the hour and the day were withheld from men. But in the pass, his natural fears had mounted higher than all his reasoning, turning into panic as he'd seen a shadowy line of Indians move along the canyon wall. In that terrible moment, with the Apaches filing down on their ponies, he'd deserted the post he'd been sent to guard. A nightmare ride had followed, and when he'd finally exhausted his horse, he'd slumped down and succumbed to sleep. He'd been awakened by rifles prodding at him and to see the accusing faces of his colleagues looking down at him. It was then that they had lit the branding fire ...

Now he reined in. The same panic was gripping him. Abel Dancer didn't want to die! But then he recalled Shane's words:

"This time you'd be betraying hundreds of people on the frontier. Just think about that as you ride on out.'

The drumming had stopped. An uncanny hush gripped the valley, broken only by the call of a coyote. The mournful sound froze him once again, but summoning what courage he had, he pushed his mount forward. He rode into a wall of darkness, not looking at the fire, not looking back at the way-station, not daring to look westwards to the trail he'd have to take if he decided to opt out.

He rode for fully five minutes, beginning to gain the glimmerings of confidence. For the first time since passing close to the Indian fire, he glanced back at their camp. It seemed mercifully distant. He'd made it! His fears were starting to leave him, and elation was spreading through his body. He only had to clear this valley and keep to the back-trails and he could make Fort Dumas. Dancer imagined the scorn on their faces when they saw him at the gates, but then he grinned as he thought how that scorn would be replaced by awe when they discovered the reason for his presence. From coward to hero! Maybe they would even want to reinstate him, but he was going to refuse. Hell, yes! He'd refuse, sure enough! The army had been ruthless with him, given him no second chance, degraded him. It had taken a man called Shane Preston to give him the chance to be born again. He began to ride faster.

Suddenly a bullet cracked out of the night, slapping squarely into his horse's head. The animal slithered into the sand in a tangle of thrashing legs, and Abel Dancer crashed with it. Desperately, he tried to grab at the gun which had fallen from his hand but even as his fingers closed over the wooden butt, half a dozen shadows fell over him and a gun-muzzle ground into his spine.

The deserter's terrified eyes slowly looked up at the ring of fierce, bronze men standing around him. He saw the pride, the anger, the triumph on their painted faces and he knew that his greatest nightmare had just begun.

A jabbering Indian stooped low and snatched the gun from his hand, and the others hauled him to his feet. All around, other Apaches seemed to rise from the very sand itself. So they had spotted him after all and staked out this ambush! He felt himself shoved from man to man as they played a sickening game with him for a few moments, a game to increase his mounting panic. Then an older warrior stopped the horseplay and barked an order. Sullenly, the braves, obeyed him and two of them thrust gun-muzzles into Dancer's back and motioned him to walk. Numb with fear, Abel Dancer falteringly went back with them over the sand, heading towards the ominous glow of their campfire.

The blaze loomed closer. He could feel its heat now, and as those in the camp saw his approach, the drumming was resumed and Indians leaped to their feet. Dancer could smell the strong aroma of cheap whisky, probably sold to them by some unscrupulous trader. He was prodded past their ponies and right into the very camp itself.

A giant of a man stood up from his blanket. He was naked except for his deerskin clout and the fire glow glistened on his chest and muscular arms. This huge figure towered head and shoulders above everyone else in the camp. His face was proud, his eyes piercing and cruel. A yellow bandanna held back the coal-black sweep of his long hair.

"I am Red Knife." The renegade leader spoke good English, a legacy of his early upbringing in a missionary's school. It was perhaps this passing interlude with whites and their ways that made him such a formidable enemy—he was an Apache, but he could think like a white man when necessary.

One of the Indians behind Dancer spoke to the chief in guttural Apache, and a slow smile formed on Red Knife's lips. Like a giant puma, he padded around to join the others behind the prisoner, and Dancer felt fingers at the back of his shirt. While at the way-station, he'd made an attempt to sew together the shreds of his shirt where the soldiers had ripped it, but his fall had opened the tears just enough for them to glimpse something of that brand. Now Red Knife's hands fastened like talons on the fabric and tore the shirt off with a single movement. The Indians whooped and jeered as they saw the brand in the firelight.

"You see, deserter-man, we have heard about you and what your friends did to you," Red Knife stated.

Still Abel Dancer said nothing.

"Come," the chief invited him.

The chief began to stalk away, but Dancer stood there, as if frozen to the sand. A savage thrust with a carbine pushed him along, and looking around at their relentless faces, Abel Dancer followed Red Knife right to the very verge of the fire. He stared at the leaping, scorching flames, aware of the renegade leader's presence beside him.

"You know how we Apaches kill our prisoners?" Red Knife asked.

There was no reply.

"The torture fire," the Indian supplied. "I can see you have already suffered the deserter's brand, but the torture fire is different. It is slow. They say a man dies many times over the torture fire."

"Dear God ...!" Dancer whispered.

"A very small fire is lit," Red Knife elaborated, "and the prisoner is hung over it from a long pole. He slowly burns—very slowly—sometimes taking all night."

Dancer closed his eyes, already feeling the pain, already imagining the vile torture he knew these Indians were capable of. Why, oh why had he been fool enough to volunteer for this mission? But it was too late for regrets now. The drumming was mounting, as if the Apaches were working themselves up into a frenzy. And he was going to provide them with perverted entertainment!

"But tonight Red Knife is willing to give deserter-man a chance to live."

Abel Dancer stared at him.

"Red Knife wants to get inside that way-station," the bronze giant grunted. "Deserter-man could help—and live!"

The former trooper looked again at the camp-fire, and Red Knife's claw-like hand fastened on his shoulder.

"White-eyes in way-station must have heard the shot, but they cannot know what happened," Red Knife said, smiling. "You will walk back to them, calling out that your horse is finished. They will open the door for you to let you in ..."

"And you will be right behind me," Dancer guessed.

"Behind you—yes," the Apache giant agreed. "But also on the other side of the way-station. You see, when you come close, the white-eyes around the back will leave their posts and run to the front. From then on, it will be easy! As for you, deserter man, you will go free. Once you have performed your task, none of my braves will touch you. You have the word of Red Knife on this!"

Dancer felt coldness creep over him. As a soldier, he'd been taught that an Indian was a born liar, but against that, he'd heard that the proud Red Knife was an exception to the rule. The renegade was regarded as a cunning, ruthless killer with an insatiable hatred for the white man, but when he spoke, his words could be relied on.

"What is it to be, deserter-man?" Red Knife demanded. "The torture-fire or freedom?"

Dancer glanced around him. His captors were watching him poker-faced. Fear-sweat broke out again, all over Abel Dancer's body. He didn't have the courage to face the torture-fire, and he knew it. Maybe he'd summoned enough courage to attempt to ride to Fort Dumas, but slow, painful dying would never be his way. The alternative was life—but a life knowing he'd betrayed his friends. Would not this be slow torture of a different kind, living in some remote border town and hearing snatches of news about innocent folks being butchered by Apaches with Beals rifles? Two alternatives! A night of hell and then merciful death—or a lifetime of hell and a lonely grave!

But maybe there was another way—if he had the guts, and even as he thought about it, Dancer wasn't sure whether he had the courage needed. He was quivering now, fighting with himself.

"Your choice, deserter-man!"

Dancer swallowed. "Tell your men to make ready," the ex-soldier croaked. "I will lead them in!"

"You are a wise man," Red Knife said.

The Indian's eyes were on fire with elation. For the first time, his hawk-like gaze now left the prisoner, and he angled around to give his braves the glad tidings.

A chorus of wild whooping rose in the night air. The drums throbbed in primitive expectation. Hands held carbines aloft to the dark sky.

Dancer hesitated. For an agonizing second his fear held him immobile. Then he whipped out his right hand, fastening on the long hunting knife in the chief's sheath. The renegade made a frantic lunge at Dancer's hand, but the deserter had already lifted the knife clear. Dancer jumped sideways, the gleaming blade clutched in his fist, and even as the Apache leader tried to grab him, he turned the knife point towards himself. Abel Dancer laughed at the renegade and then plunged the knife into his own heart. In his last dark moment, the coward had found new courage.

In a fit of rage, Red Knife gathered the lifeless, bloodied corpse into his arms. All around him, the braves were howling in dismay, cheated of torture, cheated of an easy entry into the way-station. Red Knife's eyes were hideous with hate as he lifted the body high and tossed it into the fire.

A thousand sparks flew into the sky as the corpse crashed into the fire. They rose to the stars, throwing out a vivid incandescence all over the valley. The glow grew with the sparks, playing over the top of the valley wall and illuminating a long dark line of horsemen poised on the rim, ready to swoop. The howls of rage died. Every eye was fixed hypnotically on the stark legion of riders against the firelit sky. Red Knife made a swift, sweeping count. Not twenty, but forty or more deadly silhouettes framed there! And it was the Indian chief himself who blurted out the one name even the Apaches feared.

"Mantez!"

NINE

ULTIMATUM FROM AN OUTLAW

"Mantez," Shane Preston said, as the others gathered around him at the front window. "It could only be him!"

"The red devils are runnin'!" Leif Portland cried. "Look at 'em—goin' like bats out of hell!"

John Lassetter shouted. "Then part of my prayer has been answered!"

"Whoever answered that part of your prayer has brought the devil himself to our doorstep," Jonah Jones said, quickly dampening his enthusiasm. "Me, I'd rather face Red Knife any day."

"But, don't you see?" the Mormon insisted. "If part of my prayer has been answered, then the other part will be, too."

"Keep prayin', John," Shane advised him soberly, "but also keep your cartridges handy. Could be we'll need both—and a miracle. Reckon most of you can see what I can—"

They followed his pointing finger down-valley. Beyond the fire glow a horse lay crumpled in the sand, and they all remembered the gunshot.

"If they killed his horse, they have killed him too," Shane said. "Means we won't be getting any help from Fort Dumas. Looks like it's just us against Pedro Mantez and his marauders."

"Heavens!" Cassie Portland gasped. "Look at those varmints go! I've never seen the likes of that in all my born days!"

"And well they might run," Woode commented. "There's no man, red or white, who doesn't have reason to fear the bandido, Mantez. He's looted Indian villages as well as white settlements. Even a renegade like Red Knife knows he's met his match with Mantez."

"And where does that leave us?" van Elnin demanded.

"Where we were with Red Knife," Shane told him crisply. "We're holdin' United States Army property, and the Mexican's not gonna get his paws on it."

The gambler stubbed his cigar furiously against the wall. "Now I know you're loco! Against those thirty or forty Indians at least we had a prayer, but we've no chance against that army of professional killers—because that's what they are. Cold, professional killers! When Mantez comes for us, there'll be no whooping, no drums. His men are trained raiders. They'll sneak down and fill this way-station with lead!"

"Even Mantez's bullets won't penetrate log walls," Shane told them.

"Shane," Jonah said, "this bunch will know we have those Beals—for sure."

"You're thinking what I am," Shane said grimly. "Maybe this is a case when a few civilians ought to use army property to protect that same army property."

"Couldn't have put it better myself," the oldster said. "Ammo?"

"Boxes of it to fit the rifles. Over there by the wall."

"My God!" van Elnin whined. "Are we all going to just stand by and be led by these glory-seekers? I know—you all must know—we have no chance! I say to hell with playing hero!"

"Mr. van Elnin," John Lassetter said softly, "I think I'd better start praying for you."

"Button up, you loco Mormon!" the gambler snarled. "You and your saints and your prayers! Look where they've led us—to hell!"

"I'm no religious woman," Lianna said, "but give me the Mormon's prayers any day rather than your moans and groans."

"Shane," Jonah muttered, "reckon we've got ourselves a visitor."

There wasn't an Indian left in the valley, but the dying fire glow showed Shane the long line of riders moving towards the way-station. Right out front of this line was a solitary rider, proud, alone, with a gun in his hand. Here was no ragged, unkempt scavenger of the wilderness, but a silken-shirted, flamboyant figure under a wide-brimmed sombrero. The man motioned the other riders to halt halfway between the valley wall and the trail, and then he continued alone towards the way-station. His free hand held a fluttering kerchief as a token of truce. The defenders held their fire. He reined in close to the way-station and stood in his stirrups.

"My name is Mantez!"

At the sound of the voice, Miriam clutched Shane Preston's arm, and pressed her body to his to gain strength from him. Beside her, John Lassetter was praying loudly. Woode, the former sheriff, had his arm around Lianna's waist and the 'breed girl was trembling. To most women, the very mention of Mantez brought to mind rape. It seemed that the Mexican bandido raped for the sole reason of degrading American womanhood.

Shane stepped close to the window.

"Just passing through, Mantez?" he called.

"You would wish this, hombre?" the bandido replied.

"Figured it wouldn't be a bad notion," Shane said.

Mantez sat back in his saddle. His kerchief dangled from his hand. "Señor—your name?"

"Shane Preston."

The bandido shifted in the saddle. He pushed the sombrero back on his head.

"Señor Shane Preston! I am honored! You are—what is the Americano word—famous, like me!"

"I don't figure we're in the same record book, bandido."

Mantez laughed. "I like a man with a sense of humor. But the time for joking is past. You know why we are here?"

"Why don't you spell it out?" the drifter suggested.

Mantez worked his horse around. "We had our guns stolen—would you believe it, señor?"

"Your guns?"

"I had a deal with Señor Paton—a gentleman's agreement in your lingo—by which I would pay Señor Paton a certain sum in exchange for certain guns, Beals rifles. And so, true to my word, Señor Preston, I arrive at the meeting place … a little late, I must admit, but I arrive. And what does Mantez find? Paton dead, and the tracks of a wagon leading to this place. Now, when I reached the ridge, I saw the Indians—and, I might boast, señor, my presence saved you all from the torture fire."

"We'll mail you a vote of thanks!" yelled the irrepressible Jonah, his trigger-finger itching, though he knew that one shot would bring a hail of lead from the circling bandidos.

"But there is still the matter of the guns," Mantez called out.

Shane snapped, "Those rifles are the property of the United States Army!"

"So?" Mantez shrugged.

"We're taking them back to Fort Dumas."

Mantez slowly thrust the truce kerchief inside his tunic.

"Señor Preston, how many of you are there?"

"Enough to fight you off," Shane rapped back.

The people in the way-station held their breaths.

"So be it," said Mantez, no expression in his voice. Behind him, the line of marauders was motionless, waiting like a well-trained army for the order to attack.

"Know how many hombres ride with me?" Mantez called out.

"I reckon we can count, Mantez," Shane told him crisply. "Can you count, too? I've got six shells in the gun I'm holding on you. One death in each shell, bandido."

Again, Mantez moved his horse around. "Shoot me," he said, "and you sign your own death warrant, gringo. And you know it!"

Shane was silent, hawk like eyes watching.

Mantez said, more quietly, "Hand over those rifles and I give you my word that I'll let you go free. All of you. Men—and women!"

One of the women in the way-station moaned, the others felt fear in their hearts.

Mantez said, "Well, Preston? Is it a deal?"

Shane did not hesitate. "No deal, Mantez," he said flatly.

Pedro Mantez looked up at the waning moon.

"The night is dying. When the sun comes up, you will either hand over those rifles—or die. The choice is yours."

And with that, the Mexican bandido wheeled his horse and galloped back towards his men, crouching low in the saddle.

Slowly, Shane holstered his six-gun.

"Preston! Jones!" Van Elnin's voice was shrill. Shane turned to see a black derringer in the gambler's hand.

"Put that away, tinhorn!" Shane ordered.

"This is no time for games!" Jonah warned.

"'A house divided against itself ...'" Lassetter began to quote.

"Shut up and listen—all of you!" snapped van Elnin. "I reckon I speak for every sensible person here when I say we want to live. Preston doesn't seem to give a damn, but our lives mean more to us than those pieces of wood and metal in crates—"

"Van Elnin, put away that gun!" Shane rapped again.

"Ma'am," the gambler nodded to Miriam, "you heard that Mexican. You know what he plans to do to you womenfolk—what he always does! Do I have to spell it out for you?"

"I'm saving the last bullet for myself—if the worst comes to the worst and Mantez gets inside," the girl said bravely.

"If?" said the gambler scornfully. "We've no chance, and you all know it. He'll take just two minutes to get inside here."

"He'll have to face our repeating rifles," Shane said. "We can hold out for much longer than that."

"So we hold out for an hour, maybe two or three … what then?" snarled van Elnin.

"We're not handing over those rifles," Shane snapped.

"You care more about those goddamn guns than our lives!" the gambler accused him hotly.

"I care more about hundreds, maybe thousands of other lives that those guns would end once they got into Mantez's hands," the tall drifter countered.

"What do you others think?" Jonah broke in sourly.

Van Elnin's lips twisted. "Think? They don't think! None of you think!" The gambler's voice was trembling with rage. "All of you are like sheep following this—this fool gunslinger! You'd follow him to hell itself, and that's precisely where he'll lead you! It looks like I'm going to have to save the lot of you from yourselves!"

"What do you mean?" Portland asked.

133

"I'm going to make that deal with Mantez on behalf of you all." The gambler still held the small black gun. "Later, you'll thank me—thank me for saving your lives. Right now, I intend to open that door and invite Mantez in to carry away those rifles he wants—"

"You'll have to kill me first, van Elnin," Shane said.

"That might just be a pleasure!" the gambler snarled.

Suddenly, van Elnin heard the hollow click of a gun-hammer right behind him, and moments later a hard muzzle was jabbed into his spine.

"When you pulled that derringer, tinhorn," Judson Woode said softly, "you should have looked to see if anyone was behind you. Now—drop that gun!"

"You fool, Woode!" van Elnin gasped. "You don't know what you're doing!"

"I've done a few wrong things in my life, but this ain't one of them! Now, drop that derringer, or—"

"Or you'll shoot me in the back?" Lorn van Elnin's voice had changed now to a sneer. "They say that's your style, Judd Woode! They say that's why they took your badge away in Santos—you were a back-shooting sheriff!"

Lianna's face twisted with fury and Shane Preston's eyes narrowed at the gambler's accusation.

"Oh, you figured you could ride west to escape the story. Well, Woode, being a lousy back-shooter is something you can't run from. The truth will always ride with you. There'll always be someone who knows the truth, and right here that someone happens to be me, Lorn van Elnin. So go ahead—shoot me in the back."

In a split moment of time, Woode whipped his gun high, then brought it down onto van Elnin's head with stunning force. The gambler gasped like a fish, threw back his arms and crashed to the floor.

Shane stooped and picked up the derringer.

"Thanks, Judd."

"Mebbe that tinhorn bastard was right," Woode breathed, staring at his gun.

"What do you mean, Judd?"

"A man can't run from the truth," the ex-sheriff said as Lianna came and linked her arm protectively in his.

"Was it the truth?" Shane asked quietly.

"The man was a killer," Judd said, ignoring Lianna's whispers directing him to say nothing. "I was sheriff of Santos and I knew he was in town to murder Henry Beckett—"

"Who was the killer?" Jonah wanted to know.

"Leyton Ranger."

"One of the bloodiest varmints in Texas," Jonah said frankly.

"I—I found Ranger staked out, waitin' for Beckett," Woode recalled, gulping at the memory. "I just started gunnin' and he fell dead."

"Your bullet in his back?" Shane guessed.

"Yeah."

"Henry Beckett thanked him," Lianna whispered, "and at first so did other folks. Then, when the word got around about the way Ranger died, the tongues started wagging. You know the sort of thing. 'He's just shot one man in the back. Wonder who'll get it next'?"

"So they unpinned your badge?" Shane Preston said, looking directly at Woode.

"Yeah," Woode muttered.

"But it was for more than that one back-shooting incident," Lianna spoke up defiantly to defend him. "You see, the righteous folks on the town committee hadn't exactly been pleased with Judd for some time ... because ... because of me. They figured their sheriff ought to be a lily-white god, set an example to everyone. Yet ... yet he was sleeping with a 'breed, and not even married to her. The Ranger incident gave the righteous that last bit of ammunition they needed, and now Santos has a decent, church-going, upright lawman who wouldn't know how to handle a gun but he's legally married to the mayor's daughter—a white woman, of course. Pure white."

"A lily-white god?" Jonah grinned.

"An upstanding example."

"I know those town committees," Shane remarked.

"So you decided to run from society because of that one single incident?" Jonah asked perceptively.

"From society, and from my reputation," Judd Woode said frankly. "But maybe van Elnin's showed me a man can't hide from what he really is. You see, even this far from Santos, a passenger on the third stage we boarded knew the story."

"Judd," Shane said gently, "maybe a man shouldn't try to run from his reputation but try to change it."

"And how in the hell could I do that?" the one-time badge-toter asked.

"Maybe you've started already."

"Huh?"

"You could have plugged that lousy tinhorn in the back," Shane said. "Instead you knocked him out. Just think about it, Judd—think about it between now and sunup."

"What are they doing out there?" Miriam asked him.

"Getting ready," Shane said grimly, his red-rimmed tired eyes watching over the western side of the valley.

"You know," the girl said shivering, "I think I'd rather the Indian drums to—to this silence."

"Mantez is a professional," Shane told her bluntly. "He gave us till sunrise for a reason. It gives him all night to position his men … you know, like an army general would."

"And come sunrise, they'll attack!" she exclaimed.

"See that ridge of sand?" he murmured. "Been watching it for the last hour. Mantez placed four greasers behind it. Obviously they're there to take care of this window—and me."

"I brought you another cup of coffee," she said.

He accepted the cup.

"What sort of chance do we really have?" she demanded suddenly, her hand soft on his arm.

"The odds are long, ma'am."

"What can we do?"

"We have the Beals rifles, so we'll hold out for a while. It just depends on how many of the Mexicans we can kill before they get too close for comfort. And there's just a slight chance that if we kill enough of them, Mantez will figure that the price he's paying for the guns is getting too high—and he'll quit."

"Mantez quit!" She laughed at the idea. "He'd be too proud."

"Mantez might be proud, but he's also a realist," Shane said. He sipped the steaming coffee. "Miriam, I—I hope you do what you said you'd do with your last bullet if things become hopeless."

Her hand was still on his arm. "I meant what I said, Shane. I'd die a hundred times if I was—used."

"I hope the other womenfolk have the same thing in mind as you," Shane said.

"Shane," she murmured softly, "if my ma couldn't bring herself to—to save that last bullet—would you, I mean—"

"I'm sure your pa would make sure she was taken care of," Shane Preston said.

"But if pa was dead?" She looked imploringly up at him. Shane stared down at her.

"I reckon I'd look after her, Miriam."

"Thank you," she said gratefully.

He went to raise the cup to his mouth, but Miriam's hands darted to his face and cupped his chin. Then she reached up and planted a swift kiss to his cheek. Then she stepped back, flushed.

"I—uh—reckon you'd better be taking that coffee tray around to the other rooms," Shane Preston suggested.

"Yes ... I guess I'd better," she said.

He watched her leave, and then resumed his lonely vigil at the window. A wind was rising across the valley, sweeping little puffs of sand over the trail. The campfire was now only a feeble glow, and Shane surmised that most of Mantez's fifty riders were scattered around the way-station waiting for sunrise.

He heard Judson Woode's low voice in the adjoining room, thanking Miriam for the coffee, then van Elnin's voice. The gambler had regained consciousness half an hour ago. Shane lit a cigarette. His thoughts were going over the folks inside this way-station. Some of them were running, from society, from reputations, from something else. Maybe even a decent man like John Lassetter was running from reality to a mythical paradise in Utah. Then there were the two drifters—Jonah and himself, in a way apart from accepted society. A way-station full of outcasts protecting society's guns from the bandidos! And sunrise could be the hour of destiny for many of them. Maybe all of them.

TEN

THE DEADLY
SUNRISE

For a moment it looked as though Pedro Mantez, a resplendent figure on his black horse, was the only man in the valley.

He was sitting his saddle in the gray prelude to dawn, a lonesome, motionless figure just out of range of the way-station. Not another man nor horse could be seen, but the men and women in Portland's way-station knew the bandidos were out there sure enough—concealed, waiting.

The dying moon could still be seen, a mere ghost in the sky. A solemn stillness held sway, breathless, coldly beautiful, yet holding the promise of a terrible day to come.

Shane looked down the sights of his Beals rifle. One hour ago they had opened a crate and distributed the guns and loaded them with the ammunition that had travelled with them. The rifle felt amazingly light on Shane's arm as he leveled it out at the valley.

Just then, the first pink gleam showed in the east.

It was only a glint of light, but gradually it widened and the new day dawned on the desert. Still Mantez remained motionless on his mount. But only for a few more seconds.

"Shane, the varmint's gonna pay us another call!" Jonah warned.

As insolent as a king in his own country, Pedro Mantez rode slowly towards the way-station, reining in when he was within speaking distance. By now, light was flooding the wilderness.

"Señores! Señoritas! Mantez requires your answer."

Shane cupped his mouth with his hands. "We'll see you in hell—that's our answer!"

"Then—adios, fools!" Mantez raised his arm, his fist clenched against the sky.

The valley erupted. Mexicans leaped out of the sand at the rear of the way-station and began pouring lead at the wall. The marksmen planted below the ridge beyond Shane's wall started shooting, and two bullets ripped past him and tore splinters from the woodwork. A long line of Mexicans stood up alongside twin hollows beyond the trail, and with an oath, Jonah started firing his repeating rifle.

"There goes one of the greasy varmints," Jonah cracked as his first bullet burned home into a Mexican chest.

From the eastern window, Judd Woode glimpsed two lithe figures running towards the way-station. The former sheriff raised his gun and fired three times in rapid succession. The foremost bandido plunged headlong into the sand, but even as Woode aimed again, a slug whined in from the desert and bored into his ribs. The agony was intense as he folded over the sill. The sobbing Lianna pulled him down to the floor to safety.

"The—the window ..." he warned her.

She was just in time. The other runner was almost there, his white teeth bared as he smiled in triumph a few short lengths from the window. Lianna grabbed the Beals and leveled it. She squeezed the hair-trigger and the bullet blasted into the Mexican's neck. More of them were coming and catching her breath, the girl leveled the rifle again.

Out front, Jonah was sending the Mexicans retreating for cover. Cursing, the old-timer threw down one repeating rifle and grabbed the second loaded one he'd placed beside the window. He was whooping like an Indian now as his third victim folded and crashed. "Who's next?" the oldster bellowed.

Then a screaming bullet rammed into Jonah's right arm, sending him reeling away from the window. Binnie van Elnin ran to take his place. She emptied the rifle at the bunch of men regrouping by the hollows. Behind her, a muttering Jonah Jones had tottered to his first rifle and was reloading it.

Suddenly a frantic scream came from the side bedroom.

Leaving Binnie to cope with the threat from the front, Jonah whipped out his six-gun and lunged for the passage. Clutching his wounded right arm with his other hand, Jonah barged into the bedroom. One grinning Mexican had Lianna pinned to the wall and he was systematically ripping her blouse to shreds, while another was hovering over her bloodied husband like a puma about to finish off its wounded prey. Jonah first took the one standing over Judd. His six-shooter thundered just once to blast a hole in the Mexican's head. The lecherous outlaw stripping the girl panicked. Jonah barely gave him a second longer to live, and the man sank away from the weeping girl with blood pouring from his back.

"That's one spot of back-shootin' I'm kinda proud of." Jonah quipped.

A shadow darkened the window as another marauder sought to take advantage of the unmanned post. The grin on the fat Mexican's face turned sour as Jonah calmly leveled his gun and blasted. The would-be intruder melted into the darkness of death.

"Fix Judd's wound," Jonah told the girl. "I'll watch the window."

Lianna didn't even bother to hold together her torn shreds of clothing as she ran to her man's side.

Mantez himself was directing a major offensive at the rear windows. Some ten or more marauders, this time mounted, burst through the corrals, smashing down wooden rails, streaking towards the wall that the Portlands were defending. Like a wild, dark tide, the riders surged almost to the very wall itself, right into the teeth of belching guns. With her face blackened from powder burns, Miriam fired shot after shot at the raiders. She saw two of them fall before a slug screamed out of the desert and smashed into her left breast. Darkness rose like the darkness of death itself, but as she lay in a spreading pool of her own blood beside slivers of shattered glass, she realized that death was not to be her lot right now. Bravely, she tried to claw her way up. A Mexican rode right up to the window she'd been blasted from. He leaned in through the window and her father shot him from his saddle. Miriam's vision became a blur. She could feel her mother's frantic arms around her, then a sudden jerk as Cassie Portland was struck in the face by a piece of flying glass.

Along the western wall, Shane Preston was trading lead with the Mexicans staked out behind the ridge. The three outlaws were joined by two more, and in a wave they jumped up and started running at the way-station. Shane dodged low, drawing a bead on the foremost Mexican who was brandishing an ancient carbine.

144

The Beals kicked against his shoulder, the slug plowed into the Mexican's middle and he rolled like a barrel, cannoning into the man beside him. Uncertain, the line hesitated. Two of the waverers lifted their guns as Shane's rifle boomed again. His shot winged just wide of a lean little outlaw who whipped up his rifle and fired. The tall drifter ducked and another slug whistled overhead and struck the far wall. Jabbering in Spanish, one raider surged forward to be the first one at the window. Shane waited until his dark hair showed above the sill. He aimed carefully from his position on the floor and the moment the man's whole head appeared, Shane fired. Glassy-eyed and bloodied, the face slid out of sight. Shane edged to the wall alongside the window. He heard the muffled thudding of retreating footsteps. He waited for the face which did not appear. All of a sudden, the shooting died.

Cautiously, Shane inched to the window.

He glanced out at the retreating outlaws, and the next moment, Portland burst into the room.

"We've beaten the varmints! Thank God, we've won!"

"We haven't won, Leif," Shane said dryly. "We've just shown them we're not gonna be a pushover."

"Then—then they'll be back?"

"Guess so." Shane reloaded his Beals. "What's happened? Is everyone else okay?"

"Lassetter's dead."

"Hell, no!"

"He was in the small parlor. Just called in there and he's sprawled in a pool of blood."

"Watch my window," Shane said tersely.

"And my daughter, Miriam …" Portland called out after him, "she's been hit real bad."

Shane strode through into the parlor. The window had been smashed. Crockery had been swept off the table where John Lassetter's body had crashed before finally crumpling to the floor. There was a dark pool of blood around the Mormon's head.

The tall drifter knelt down, his fingers probing through the oozing blood for the wound.

"Maybe he damn well has got the angels with him!" Shane forced a quick grin. "The Bible-thumper's only been creased."

It was dark in the cellar—and cold.

But it had been a relatively safe place while the guns were thundering.

And yet it wasn't going to be safe for long. Lorn van Elnin told himself that as he levered himself up from the damp floor. The next time Mantez's raiders came they'd overwhelm these fools who stood against them, and then they'd comb the entire place. Even the cellar. If they found him here, unarmed even, they'd still assume he'd gone along with Preston's crazy scheme to prevent those rifles falling into their hands.

His only chance to live was for Mantez to know the truth. He'd opposed Shane Preston's fool notion—yes, bitterly opposed it, even suffered a gun-smash on the back of his head for his heroic stand against the insane drifter. Mantez had to know this, but he'd have to know well before the final onslaught when blood-crazed Mexicans breached the defenses and couldn't distinguish between the fools and him.

Mantez would have to know now!

The gambler ran the back of his hand over his stubbled chin. It shouldn't be too hard to convince the bandido during this lull in the battle. After all, van Elnin reasoned, the moment Mantez saw him riding out there with his hands raised high in surrender, he'd realize that here was a defector.

The gambler began to climb up the wooden ladder to the storeroom. He pushed open the hatch and crawled out. He could hear folks running around, but right now they wouldn't be worried about him—they had things to attend to, like tending wounds and getting ready for the next attack.

Lorn van Elnin scrambled to the passage door.

He edged outside. What about his wife, Binnie? He didn't afford her a second thought. She'd had her chance to stand by him, and she'd chosen to act like a fool. Well, let her die with the rest of them. Women like her were two a penny in border towns. All he needed to do was start winning at the tables and they'd flock to him.

But first he had to get out of this hole. He ran to the rear door. He glimpsed Cassie Portland out of the corner of his eye, but she was reaching for some bandages and didn't even notice him. Quietly, he unlatched the door.

The gambler jumped outside, his boot squelching on the pulpy flesh of a dead Mexican. He sniffed distastefully before starting to walk out into the desert. He passed the stable and kept going, his hands raised high to heaven, a white, flapping kerchief in his right hand. A couple of startled Mexicans spotted him.

"Mantez!" van Elnin called out confidently. "Mantez—I'm your friend—your amigo. Do you hear, Mantez? Amigo!"

At the sound of his hoarse, pleading voice, faces appeared at the rear windows and the Mexicans seemed to leap out of the sand. Between the two opposing forces, van Elnin kept walking in his chosen direction.

"Hey! Come back, you crazy loon!" Jonah yelled.

"Lorn! Lorn!" Binnie screamed. Any love for her gambling husband had long since died, but seeing him walk out like that brought sudden terror to her throat.

"You damn fool—come back, while you can!" Portland roared.

But van Elnin ignored them.

Three Mexicans drew alongside him, guns drawn. More were closing in. He saw the big black horse and its haughty rider approach, then remain motionless, waiting for him.

The gambler's face wore sweat and a smile. He joked in poor Spanish with the stony-faced Mexicans who surrounded him, escorting him to Mantez's stirrup. He looked right up at the face looming over him like an olive sun.

"Señor Mantez—you must listen to me," he began. "Remember when … you came last night … to the porch … and gave out that very fair offer of yours? Of course you do! Of course! Well, I was one who didn't agree with what Shane Preston said. They … they chose to fight. All except me. I waited for this chance to come out to join you, my amigo. Not that it was easy. Not easy indeed! I had to sneak out … yes, actually sneak out, because they would have killed me for joining you, my friend, my amigo! You want proof I was against them? Look at my head! Yes, please look … you'll see a bump … one hell of a bump … a blow from a gun struck at me while I was trying to persuade them to listen to reason and accept your reasonable offer—please look at my head, feel it if you like. Yes, feel it. Please. It proves my story. Now, please, señor, may I have the privilege of telling you how you can take that way-station a little easier? Isn't that proof I'm your amigo? Ah, yes. You believe me, don't you … I can see that now … that's so good …"

There was a smile on Mantez's face, and van Elnin was so hypnotized by that smile that he didn't see the gun. But he heard the hammer being clicked back.

"Amigo ... amigo ..." van Elnin whimpered frantically.

The gun spat and a bullet tore a crater right in the center of the gambler's head.

ELEVEN

ONE HUNDRED GUNS

"Hold still, Miriam, and take a swig of some of Jonah's redeye," Shane Preston said, sitting beside her on the bed. "It's a mite stronger than the brew your pa keeps."

The girl's trembling lips opened for the pain-deadener which Jonah helped her drink down. In pain yet already feeling some relief, she looked up at Shane with trusting eyes.

There were several wounds to be tended, but Shane had judged this one to be the most urgent. The bullet was lodged high in her left breast, and already Miriam had lost a lot of blood.

"I'm no medic, Miriam," Shane told her, "but one thing I do know. This is a mite too close to your heart for comfort."

"I—I want you—to take it—out," she breathed, blood on her lips.

"Lie still," he told her. "Jonah—the knife been boiled?"

"As boiled as it'll ever be," Jonah said, fetching the knife from the open front of the wood stove.

Cassie Portland, her face cut by the flying glass, stood by as Jonah carried the knife to the tall drifter.

"Try not to worry, ma'am," Jonah Jones said, trying to reassure the portly woman. "My partner's sure done this before—many times, in fact, even to me."

"Dear God." She buried her face in her hands as the knife moved towards her daughter's tender breast.

Jonah thrust a wooden spoon between Miriam's teeth and she bit on it like a clamp.

Shane began to probe.

"Please, God ... help him, help her ..." Cassie wept, her face now buried against Jonah's barrel chest.

Two minutes passed. Two minutes of agony numbed by the whisky.

"What's—what's happening?" Cassie Portland whispered against old Jonah. "I can't look."

"He's nearly there, ma'am."

Shane found the bullet. It wasn't in as deep as some he'd been called upon to cut out in an emergency, but it was deep enough. He began to lever out the lethal lead. Seconds later the Mexican slug was on the floor. Shane said nothing as he plugged the wound after first dabbing it with spirit. Then he nodded to Cassie.

"She's all yours, ma'am. Bandage her well and then follow me into the next room. We'll need a bandage for John Lassetter's head and Woode's side. And don't fret if Miriam doesn't speak to you … she went right out to it when my knife found the bullet."

Shane went through to the next room, which resembled one of the makeshift hospitals he'd known when soldiering with Tom Cannell in the war. Judd Woode was leaning against the wall, a makeshift bandage around his middle. The bullet which had plowed into his ribcage had mercifully ripped right on through and out, leaving two wounds to be sterilized and tended, but no slug to probe for. Lassetter sat on the floor in a daze, nursing his head. Jonah too, had a wounded arm which ought to have been looked at, but the oldster muttered that he was tough enough to see out this battle.

The tall Texan looked at them proudly. They were outcasts, some of them. Some of them were wounded. Yet they had held off the most powerful bandido bunch Mexico had ever spawned!

But how much longer could they hold out?

"Shane!" It was Binnie.

He ran to the window, joining the tearful widow as she stood guard.

"Look—they're coming—all together this time—straight for the front porch—thirty, maybe forty of the Mexicans."

"Creepin' Moses!" Jonah was grim-faced. "All in one big bunch."

"Reckon this is it," Leif Portland whispered fearfully.

"They're coming at us together—we face them together," Shane announced. "Everyone to the front room."

They ran, walked or shuffled to the main room.

Shane edged open the front door. The bandido army was approaching in a solid mass, every man on his horse and clutching a gun. Even Shane's throat went suddenly dry as he realized that all of them were facing cold death. Pedro Mantez was leading the Mexicans, his black horse magnificent, and the bandido looking like a general in the saddle.

"This is it, ain't it, Shane?" Jonah growled beside him.

Shane said nothing.

On came the riders, hoofs beating a muffled drum of death.

Then Pedro Mantez reined in and the raiders sat saddle behind him. The bandido raised his gloved hand in the traditional American salute. "I am paying you all a tribute. This is because you are not like that yellow fox I just shot dead. You have been brave, very brave. And because of this, I am giving you one last chance to see reason before I give the word to ride in and kill. Hand over those guns—and you live."

Shane felt his throat go even drier. He thought about Miriam, so vulnerable in her wounded condition. In fact, over half of them had been wounded and were really in no condition to fight. And yet, they were so few compared with others who would suffer if Mantez had his way.

"No one could blame you, amigo."

Shane still said nothing.

"You have one minute. Then, Pedro Mantez will give the word which will mean your death …"

The seconds ticked away. Agonizing seconds. The seconds of life itself.

"We can't yield," Shane said.

"Ten seconds," the bandido said.

Shane stepped back inside. He slammed the door.

Suddenly, John Lassetter's face glowed like a lamp. He clutched his hands together, raising them to heaven as he stood beside one of the front windows.

"We're saved!" the Mormon yelled.

"The Bible-boy's delirious," Jonah scoffed. "Check your guns, everyone!"

"No, we're saved!" John Lassetter croaked. "Look on the valley ridge—the saints are coming! Praise the Lord—He sent the saints!"

Shane joined him at the window.

"Wagons!" the drifter cried elatedly. "Wagons— dozens of them heading this way! I don't know whether they're saints or sinners riding in them, but by the powers, they're toting guns!"

The Mexicans wheeled their horses as the cavalcade bore down upon them, more than forty wagons, loaded with men carrying guns.

"The saints! The saints!" Lassetter was babbling. "They're my people, Shane! The wagon-train I somehow missed ..."

"And they must have heard the gun battle and came to investigate," Shane Preston supplied.

"The Lord sent them," the Mormon insisted.

"And I for one won't argue with you," Shane said with a smile.

The Mexicans were fleeing now, turning their mounts and plunging west as the Mormon pioneers opened fire. Five raiders fell in the first fusillade. Another slumped forward in the saddle.

Shane grabbed up his rifle. He ran outside, squinting down the sights at one man who hadn't budged and who simply sat saddle, speechless with rage. Mantez stared at the oncoming wagons, his eyes on fire with seething anger and sheer disbelief. It was as if his prey had been plucked from his talons! Stunned by hate, Mantez slowly leveled his rifle at the foremost wagoner.

"Mantez!" Shane called out above the din of churning wagon wheels and the distant booming of gunfire.

The bandido swung around, trying to vent his terrible fury on Shane Preston now as he brought up his gun. Shane fired, just beating the bandido's trigger finger, and the rifle bullet seared across the sand to smash into the Mexican's heart. Mantez swayed in the saddle and collapsed to the desert floor, and moments later dust swirled over him as the first wagon rumbled by and two bearded Mormons turned the horses towards the way-station. Shane Preston stood there and after a moment grinned as he read the painted slogans on the canvas sides of the wagons that were lining up before them all. SALT LAKE CITY OR BUST! THE LORD'S SAINTS! ANGELS WATCH OVER US! ONWARD TO PARADISE!

"Know something, Shane?" Jonah almost wept beside him. "You can call me a Mormon-lover as of now!"

"John's gone," Shane said, handing Miriam her coffee. "Gone with the folks he said he missed. Only he hadn't missed them at all. They hadn't even arrived when he got himself lost around Alkali Flat. They were still on their way through, and luckily for us, they came this way. Heard the gunfire and decided to investigate."

"John was telling me about this visitation he had …" Miriam frowned.

"I warned him not to preach to you!"

"But he did."

"Anyhow, concerning that visitation," Shane said, "I seem to recall some angel was supposed to have

157

told him to stay with us for a while. Well, if that same angel brought those—uh—saints, as he called them, I'd sure like him on my side and not against me!"

"You thinking of becoming a Mormon?"

"No, ma'am," he said. "I figure one wife's enough for any ordinary man."

"Oh," she murmured seriously. "But—but you won't be looking for one until you find … Scarface."

"That's right," he said, aware once more of his mission and that other trails, other places, would soon be calling him.

"Shane …"

"Yeah?"

"After you've found him, and decide to settle down, will you remember the girl at Portland's way-station?" Miriam asked. "And—and will you call by?"

"Reckon I might."

"I'd like to give you a reason to," Miriam Portland said softly. She had been weakened by her wound, but nevertheless, she summoned the strength to reach up and pull his face down to hers. Then she pressed her full lips to his. "There, Shane Preston—that's the reason why you ought to remember—and call by."

"So long, Miriam."

And then he left her.

As he saddled his palomino, Snowfire, he glanced back at Binnie van Elnin. Now she was alone, but then, as she'd explained to him a few minutes ago, maybe she'd always been alone living with Lorn.

"Make sure you take him straight to a medic," Shane advised Lianna as he saw the ex-lawman and his girl about to leave on the stage she was going to drive herself. "The west wouldn't want to lose a candidate for a law office."

"How's that again?" Woode gasped.

"You think about it," Shane smiled.

And then he was heading away to where Jonah was waiting for him astride old Tessie.

"Gentlemen," Major Cannell said, shaking their hands, "the United States Army is in your debt. You will find a check in this envelope together with an order which entitles you to retain two of those Beals rifles."

Jonah raised his eyebrows. He already had one in his saddle-scabbard.

"Glad to be of help, Tom," Shane said sincerely. "I'm just sorry we can't take you up on your other offer."

"A pity … a pity …" The major shook his head. "You two would have made fine, upstanding scouts on our full time payroll."

"I just can't be tied down, Tom. Guess you know why."

"Sure."

"We'll be moving along now," Shane said, shaking Cannell's hand once more.

"Before you leave, I've just remembered something." There was a strange smile on the soldier's face, and it was directed at the whiskered drifter. "Yes, something very important."

"Something to do with me? Like some free redeye, for instance?" Jonah ventured.

"It has something to do with you, Jonah, but it's nothing to do with drinking. While you were away, a certain lady rode to the fort asking after you."

"After me?" Jonah feigned complete innocence.

"Her name's Helen."

"Creepin' Moses!" Jonah gasped.

"Said she was concerned about your general welfare for a very, very special reason. She claimed you and her were about to embark on the matrimony trail."

"Hell, no!"

"She's here, staying over in the visitors' quarters for women," Cannell informed him.

"Here … now?" Jonah looked like he'd been stung by a bee.

It took Jonah Jones just ten seconds flat to be mounted on Tessie and out of the gates of Fort Dumas. And then he didn't stop riding the mare until he was well clear of the military outpost.

Shane found him when he finally took his leave of Cannell and followed Jonah's trail to a little canyon.

"Are you spooked by a female?" Shane teased him.

"Nope," Jonah snorted, mopping his sweating brow, "I'm just all-fired anxious for us to get onto the trail of that Scarface feller you're always on about. Let's ride, Shane."